OUT OF MY
BRAIN

SHORT STORIES

R.D. McKown

authorHOUSE®

AuthorHouse™
1663 Liberty Drive
Bloomington, IN 47403
www.authorhouse.com
Phone: 1 (800) 839-8640

Published by AuthorHouse 03/04/2016

ISBN: 978-1-5049-8434-8 (sc)
ISBN: 978-1-5049-8433-1 (e)

CONTENTS

Chapter I

HAPPY DEATHDAY

Jeffry Coffy hurried down the road, looking about. "Good", he thought the other children had not followed him. He was tired of their hateful taunts, and rock throwing antics. "Mutant," they **had** screamed at him, as they hobbled after him, with their twisted bodies straining to keep up with him. ...to destroy what they feared, and felt repelled by it. Jeffry could possibly be the only child in the state, or even in this country, who was immune to disease. In the last hundred years, due to pollution of the earth's ozone layer, most children were born with defects of some kind. This was the year 2205 A.D., and Jeffry was the only child who didn't even catch the common cold. Unfortunately, his peers treated him like a freak. Some of the children had defects, like Cerebral Palsy, and others had a variety of breathing disorders, forcing them to wear portable respirators, to breathe with. The air was very thin, but it didn't slow Jeffry down one bit. Jeffry knew the words for these children who hated him much...jealously!

Jealously! Yes! That was it! They wanted to be able to run, jump, and play without stumbling over their twisted bodies. It was not his wish to be different than anybody else. HE dreaded living home every day. Jeffry raced down the hill, his long brown hair trailing in the breeze, his long legs pumping faster on the incline. He arrived at home, tired from his running. He was relieved he had made it safely, without any confrontation with the others. He stumbled in to the front room, and unloaded his back pack full of schoolbooks on the couch.

His father sat slumped in front of the video screen, using his portable respirator gasping in grateful amounts of air. Jeffry gazed at his father, a pitiful sight of flesh. "How was your day son?" he said, between his raggedy breaths. "Nothing new, dad, He commented, heading upstairs to his room. His mother appeared from the kitchen. "How are you, honey? "She queried. She sat at the table, sipping her afternoon tea, the heat rising up from the cup, in drifts of steam. Jeffry entered the kitchen, on second thought, heading for the fridge, looking for something cool to drink. "Ok, mom". His mother sighed sadly, and then got up to make another cup of tea. JEFFRY Watched, as his mother dragged her club foot around with her. **A birth defect**, she never allowed it to interfere with her housework.

A savage purplish mark of disease was well hidden on her forehead, as she combed lustrous blonde hair over it. Even in this day and age, a woman must have some part of vanity. Jeffry felt a pang of sadness in his heart. Embarrassed by his own good health, he offered, "Want some help, mom? "No that's all right, son", she replied, pouring another cup of tea, and dragged her deformed limb back to the table. His sister Lindy crept into the kitchen. Lindy was born with one leg shorter than the other, and a cleft lip, which made her speech slurred, as she spoke, "Theffry,", she slurred, "Howth it goingth". She moved across the floor slowly, her leg brace, creeping loudly. Lindy could be a real pain in the butt at times, but apparently, today wasn't it. The grimace of pain on her face was enough to know her leg was bothering her again. She reached down, and pulled up a chair to sit in, making a white mask of pain in doing so. She lowered herself in to it, shaking. Jeffry's' father called out in a raspy voice, "The lotto is coming on, now". The lottery ran once a week. Every week on someone's birthday, and individual was selected for termination. This was a privilege to die. Considering the suffering most people went through, it was a blessing! Everyone in the house gathered round the video screen that projected its image onto the front room wall.

The three-d image collaged, then merged, revealing a man with his respirator on, a built in mike attached to his mask. HE Was dressed flamboyantly in a red and green checkered suit, prevalent among sports announcers of that time. His voice boomed rasping, like that of a rusty nail being scraped across concrete. "It's time to play… Happy Death day",. As he spoke, a crowd of people mimicked him in the same words, echoing though the vid screen to its audience. The announcers voice continued merrily, "Who shall be our lucky participate today? The announcer looked down upon the computer in front of him. He punched into the computer's memory banks. The machine lit up, its many colored lights flashing in several rows of brilliance. It whirled, then stopped, spitting out its info. "And the winner is… Jeffry Coffy, of Wichita Kansas! All eyes in the room turned towards him. Jeffrys' heart froze! His head spun dizzily, and then he gratefully passed out, on the floor. Jeffry dreamed or was it real! He was running, running for his life.

The other children were chasing him. He moved in slow motion, barely getting away from them. Then he stumbled, pitching forward on his face, into the dirt. THEY swooped upon him, like hungry vultures for a meal. They surrounded him, leaving no avenue of escape. "We got you now mutant', called a voice from the crowd. One child leaned forward,. It was Lindy, his sister! "Got to get you ready for death day", she smiled malevolently, producing a bone saw from behind her back. She continued, "Now when were done with you, you'll, want to die".

As Jeffry opened his mouth to scream, they descended upon him with hammers, knives, and other implements of torture. Lindy smiled, as she cut through bone, and cartilage. "This should make us even", she laughed. Jeffry screamed once, as Lindy grinned, sawing through his legs, blood gushing out in torrents. Jeffry awoke, beads of sweat running in rivulets down from his face, onto his chest. Shaking his head, he realized he was in his own bed. He then knew, his parents had somehow dragged him upstairs to his room. Setting up, he strained his ears for any sounds within the house. Nothing! He crept out of bed slowly. He padded slowly out of the room, and down the hall towards the kitchen. He could hear voices coming from it, but was barely able to hear the words. Jeffry crept closer to hear. "Why couldn't it be me? his sister moaned. "Now now", his mother replied gently. "That's a good question", his father stated, "The boy is disgustingly healthy". "WHY INDEED", Jeffry thought to himself". Only one person could answer that question, He must go and see his science teacher, Professor Gottman but not tonight! No, tonight the family may be checking up on him. He had till the day after, on his sixteenth birthday...Then oblivion!

Jeffry sneaked back in to bed. He wouldn't be getting any sleep tonight. He closed his eyes, but demonic visages' impaled him to no end. At almost dawn, he snoozed briefly. then the vid screen lit up, announcing, "Get up, get up, It's time for class! Jeffry snarled something obscene at the screen. He then got up and dressed for school. At breakfast, no one said a word about last night. His sister just glared at him, jealously in her eyes. His father talked on about his work. His mother though, Jeffry caught a tear in her eye. A look of worry in her usually tranquil face. Yes he wasn't the only one worried about tomorrow then. Jeffry hurried off to school. Today was to be a field trip to the old museum on Pawnee street. Jeffry disliked these excursions.

Most often, the class was allowed to destroy and artifact of beauty. Destroying that which could never be... normal! This made Jeffry sad. As he arrived at the school, the robot-buses were waiting to load the children. The teacher, Miss Ames, called to him impatiently. "Hurry Jeffry or you'll miss the fun! "Some fun, Jeffry thought, destruction of our national treasures. "It was best to keep these thoughts to himself. You never knew who might turn you in to the secret police, for…Evaluation! Or maybe worse! He had heard of such things happening, but had never seen it in person. Best not to ever find out. "But what the hell, tomorrow, I could be dead".

He boarded the bus with the others. Matt, one of his classmates, who had a hunchback, and one good eye, approached him. Jeffry steeled himself for a verbal attack. That was easier then to get away with a physical confrontation. It could always be denied, on the grounds that mutants would lie about it to get attention. Matt's intentions turned out to be casual, almost friendly. "Hey Jeffry, he smiled, "I heard you won the lotto". Jeffry merely nodded, waiting. Matt stuck out his hand to him. Jeffry eyed it suspiciously. "Hey! Matt deferred, "its o.k., your one of us now!' He smiled, winking his one eye at Jeffry. With a sigh of relief, Jeffry accepted matt's hand. "We are all with you bud", he continued, "a little envious, too". With that, he returned to his seat.

Others turned around and gave him a smile. "Maybe today wouldn't be so bad after all", he thought. Then he remembered. Matt had said, "One of us". He shuddered, remembering the dream of the night before. "Never, he thought, shaking his head vigorously. The bus came to a stop. They were here, at the museum! They all exited, as the robot-bus announced their departure. Swinging the mechanical doors open, they hobbled, slid, and waddled out, except for Jeffry, who waited last to exit. The last time he didn't, he almost ran over a few of them. He exited slowly, not wanting to attract any ones attention. They all piled through the doors of the museum. Jeffry gaped about the place. Long in disuse, the museum had once been a thriving place, two hundred years ago. Paintings of glorious colors, red, green, and purple, assailed his senses! As Jeffry admired the place, the curator stepped out handling a painting. But what a masterpiece of a painting! Beautiful, in its gold framing.

The picture depicted a mother, radiant of the birth of her child. The child, just born, appeared serene and calm. Many people had gathered around the two, and animals appeared in the back ground. The two, mother and child, looked peaceful! They looked, so perfect! Kind of other worldly. The curator left the piece standing up, propped by and old table in the center of the room. All the children, fascinated, glanced upon it briefly.

"Now children, Miss Aimes hissed softly, "DO IT". The children, fifteen in all, swooped down on the painting, ready to rend and destroy it! Jeffry hesitated in awe. The children pulled, kicked, and punched, vying for a piece of the painting. The sight made Jeffry's stomach, lurch, and rebel. Matt, not to be outdone by his peers, dropped his pants and defecated on portions of the picture, all but obliterating it.

The spray also hit a few others, who cursed at him. then continued their rampage, stripping and shedding the wondrous colors, stomping it into a thousand pieces. Jeffry sickened by it, turned away. Out of the corner of his eye, he spotted Miss Aimes, scolding matt. "Not appropriate in public. She whispered softly to him, "nice touch, and son". Jeffry moaned, as the heat began to rise up, in gorges, from his stomach and his throat. Miss Aimes spied him preparing to leave. She reached him in three quick strides. Gripping his arm, she attempted to pull him back towards the group. But Jeffry's' stomach wouldn't have any of this.

As Miss Aimes opened her mouth to admonish him, Jeffry opened his, exploding a torrent of fluids upon her dress, and in her hair. The woman shrieked, letting go of Jeffry. Jeffry ran, still vomiting, out the door and down the street. Miss Aimes, touching her hair, now a congealed mess, pulled her wig off, revealing her diseased head, pock marked with scars, and broken blood vessels. The children gaped at her. "Not funny", she mumbled to no one in particular. "Not funny at all", she shouted. "Damn you, Jeffry", she screeched, making the children cringe as she shouted more curses. "Damn mutant", she whispered. Jeffry ran down the street, almost toppling over one individual passing by, on his way to work. He collided with the man, knocking his respirator loose from his face.

The man gasped for air, grappling at the mask. He cursed Jeffry in ragged breaths. Jeffry regained his stride, and ducked down an alley just three blocks away from the museum. Jeffry attempted to catch his breath. He paused, leaning up against a wall, which had bordered slogans painted on it. The anti-graffiti squad must have missed this one, he thought. Continuing down the alley, he almost tripped over a prone body there, curled up in a fetal position near a waste disposal unit. Jeffry halted, but still contacted the body with his feet.

The body jerked to; life. With a start. "What the fuck", he bellowed. Jeffry recovered his surprise, and then stepped back from the belligerent man, still cursing at him. "Sorry", Jeffry said, then stepped closer to the man.

The man rose up on his feet, wobbling. "Who the hell are you running from kid? Jeffry shook his head. 'Myself, I guess". 'Hell kid, the man laughed, "Aren't we all". The man clasped Jeffry's' shoulder. Jeffry stepped back, unsure of this stranger. "It's ok, kid, the man smiled again, "you're welcome to my domain". The man squatted down near the waste unit, and gestured to Jeffry to do the same. Hesitatingly, Jeffry squatted down too. "Don't worry kid, the man said, "No one is sane enough to come back here". Jeffry looked at the man puzzled. The man laughed, and then coughed violently. The cough lasted a few seconds then passed. He cleared his throat. "I was once an assistant librarian, if you can believe it". Jeffry shook his head. "Really, the man insisted. He continued, "The state censored everything, and burned the libraries". Jeffry sat, entranced by the man's' speech. "I was forced from my job physically, and then sent to a reeducation center for malcontents". Here he paused, coughing up clots of blood. "Sorry, the man said, then spoke further.

"I was one of the few who had been born normal!' Jeffry looked surprised. "Yes, the man stated, "I don't look healthy now, the state took care of that". Jeffry shook his head again. "Believe it or not, kid. "When they found out I was healthy normal I would say, they injected me with a Tuberculin virus ". Jeffry looked shocked. 'yes, it's true", the man said rolling up his sleeve, revealing a scar on his upper forearm. Jeffry speechless, could only stare. "And when that wasn't enough", the man glared, "They amputated my leg below the knee, so I couldn't run very far." In a dramatic gesture, the man pulled up his right pants leg, revealing a stainless steel prosthesis running from the man's, to his foot, which was also made of some type of alloy. "But why...Why did they do this? Jeffry finally spoke up, his eyes bulging with horror.

The man merely returned him a sad smile, then remarked, "The status quo, kid, the status quo". "So everyone could be a freak, that way no one would be different". "That way nothing would upset the power structure of the state".

He continued, "People would revolt, then the state structure would topple like dominos". "Don't you see?" Jeffry understood to well. Now the state wanted to eradicate him, to maintain the status quo. There must be a way out! As if reading his thoughts, the man spoke up. "Buck up, kid, the man grinned, "Run, run, like hell"." Run, run, where? Jeffry asked. The man sat thinking for a moment, and then stood up slowly, his prosthesis creaking. "Damn thing", he commented, reaching down to realign his leg. "At least they could give me one that works!" "Give me a hand, kid, the man pointed at the waste unit.

Curious, Jeffry stepped up to him. "Push like this", the man instructed, shoving hard against the unit. Jeffry complied; the both of them shoved the unit backwards. A clank of heavy metal straining assaulted their ears, and then to Jeffry's' amazement, the unit gave way. It gave way, swinging to the left, revealing a passageway, and tunnel through the wall. "This way", the man volunteered, entering the passage. Jeffry gazed in. It looked dark and sinister. The man noted his hesitation. 'Hell kid, what could a cripple do to you?" Jeffry steeled himself, stepped in, and followed the man. They entered a long tunnel. It was dark! The man reached into his coat pocket, producing a laser light. The light was weak, and slightly inflectional. Still, they could see where they were going. In a few minutes, they had arrived. A room! A room bathed in magnificent brilliance! Jeffry squinted his eyes. The man stepped into the room, gesturing to Jeffry to do the same. Jeffry entered the room. Looking about, he spied a bookshelf! With several rows of books! Excited, Jeffry crossed the room and gazed fondly at the literature there.

Never in his life had he seen so many books! He touched several of them briefly. "Nice huh? questioned the man. He sat resting on a cot made of steel. "Look at the third book from the end, the man said, "I think it will help you marvelously". Jeffry grasped the book in question. Slowly dusting off the cover, he read "Civil Disobedience, by, he could barely see the name...Thoreau. "You can stay as long as you like", the man said, yawning. "Read that", he continued, stretching out on the cot. "I'm going to take a nap". Jeffry sat down on the hard brick floor, and began to read. Soon, though, he dozed off, drifting into a peaceful sleep. He awoke with a start, looking around, trying to pinpoint where he was.

Then he remembered. The man was sitting on the cot, looking at him. "Get a good rest, boy", he asked. Jeffry nodded. "Good, good, ", the man said. "Why were you running?" the man asked. I Jeffry explained the whole story to him. Somehow, he trusted the man. He told him about the lotto, and the incident at the museum.

The man shook his head in wonder. Then the man said, "The status quo, boy, they want to get rid of you". "But why", Jeffry asked. "Why not reeducate me, and mutilate like you?" "The man rose up from his cot. "There's something special about you, boy". "I don't know what, but it scares the state, and that's why they want to get rid of you". "How can I find out?" Jeffry asked. The man replied, there is one way, he paused, "I know someone who can help you". "You must follow my instructions close". Jeffry nodded his head. Having nothing to lose now!

The man stepped forward. "Follow the tunnel back for a hundred yards, then turn left, and continue till you come to a fork in the tunnel". Take a right at the fork". "Knock three times on the wall closet to you. "There somebody will help you". "Aren't you going with me"? Jeffry asked. The man shrugged his shoulders. "I am too screwed up". "Besides, it's time for my fix". With that, he produced a needle gun from under the bed. Fascinated, Jeffry watched him load a tube into it. Real-Itol! That's what it is! A hallucinogenic drug banned fifty years ago. It had been originally made for people who could not handle the reality of their deformaties.

The drug made you..Well, uncaring, relaxed. Perception was distorted, the whole world looked beautiful, and nothing could spoil it. Unfortunately, in eight hours the drug wore off, leaving the user in deep depression. After the states reality brainwashing, they banned the drug, too many suicides preceded the let down of the withdrawal. "That's Illegal ", Jeffry commented, watching the man shoot up. The man smiled, then withdrew the gun, "Nothing is illegal if the state allows it". He continued, "The state issues us reeducated people the luxury of the drug, so they won't have any nasty suicides, on their hands, because we couldn't handle being deformed by them". Jeffry just stared, no longer shocked at anything he heard now. "Go on. Son," the man said. sinking down on his cot. "Someone will help you there". "I'm beyond help", he moaned. The man waved the boy on. Jeffry turned to leave.

The man mumbled, as Jeffry left. "If those sobs' come to get me, I'll blow them a great big kiss, then kicked the robots in their iron crotches". He laughed. Unsure, but definitely no way out now, Jeffry continued to the tunnel, following the man's' instructions. He came to the spot the man had told him to knock on. He hammered on the wall three times. He waited. Then he heard the sound of the wall creaking as it turned. The wall section swung open wide, emitting a beam of light, exploding into Jeffry's eyes. He then rubbed them, trying to get the glare out of his pupils. A voice said quietly, "come in Jeffry, I've been expecting you". That voice! It was oddly familiar! Recovering his sight, Jeffry's mind churned the sound of the voice over in his mind. "That's it, Jeffry spoke, "Professor Gottman, my science teacher." Jeffry stepped forward, out of the dark, into the light. He blinked several times, adjusting his eyes. He was in a narrow hallway, where his teacher stood, clad in his pajamas. "Come in boy", Gottman smiled, gesturing to him. The professor, about sixty years old, greeted him. He walked towards Jeffry, with a slight limp, and his breathing

18

like a train pushing up an incline. His thinning grey hair was mussed, as if had just awoke. He escorted Jeffry into the large living area. Jeffry started in surprise! Something was missing! Then he glanced up on the wall. No vid screen! No evidence of one at all. Gottman smiled, almost reading Jeffry's mind. He stated, "Don't believe in the idiot box, bad for the brain". "Please sit down, ", he offered, pointing to a maroon love seat stationed at the other side of the room. Jeffry glanced around. There on the walls hung real paintings! Also a large book case with several hundred books! "Quite a treasure" said Gottman smiling, "I collect the past".

He continued, clearing his throat. "But you are here to solve your dilemma, now". "Yes, I am, ", Jeffry spoke confidently. "It was only a matter of time before they got to you", Guttmann explained. "How do you mean that"? asked Jeffry fidgeting nervously on the love seat. "You know, Gottman started, "if they get rid of you it will make them feel safer". "No one will remember what its' like to be a normal person. ""Yes I know that"< Jeffry answered. "What else? Guttmann cleared his throat again. "You are one of a kind, they think". He continued further. "You, Jeffry, have the immune gene in your body, to help save this country from dying out". Jeffry sat in stunned silence. He swallowed hard once, and then spoke up. "Professor, "you said, they think, are there others like me? "Yes, the professor replied, "a few scattered about the country". He went on, explaining, "There is a group outside the city in hiding, right now!" I must see them! Jeffry declared, getting up. "Easy boy, said Guttmann, restraining Jeffry by the arm. "We must not let the government suspect you". "The hardest thing you can do is go through the death lotto, as predicted". "What!" Jeffry started, stepping back, almost falling over the love seat. "I have something to show you, Gottman replied. Gently. "Wait here".

Gottman exited the room, returning with a small metallic silvery object that slightly resembled a watch. "I am already sixty years old and dying of tuberculosis". He continued, "What happens to me does not matter, he sighed. "But for the human race to exist, we must save you". "There for, he paused; we must not let them know you are going to ruin their little game for them tomorrow, with this". HE extended his hand forward, giving the object to Jeffry. "What is it? Jeffry asked, turning the object in his hand. It did resemble a watch, but that was all. There were several digits in series of tens on the face of it, and a few calibration numbers Jeffry could only guess at. "A micro-chip scrambler that will block signals from any electronic device, the same the game uses", Gottman explained. Just press this...He indicated to the second hand and it will jam their signals, allowing you to escape. He smiled, "Trust me". Jeffry looked doubtful. "Try it at home, on something simple", Gottman suggested. Jeffry tucked the scrambler into his jeans pocket. "You must leave now", Gottman stated, before any one catches us together". "But how will I know...Jeffry began. Gottman interjected "you'll be contacted at the game". He continued, "We have a man there that will get you out". "Now go, son, he urged, "Before we're spotted".

They walked through the huge living area, till they came to a door in the rear of the house. "A back door! Jeffry exclaimed. Gottman smiled, "one of the older houses, most new dwellings has. "It's easier to catch people with out and escape route. Jeffry nodded. Gottman reached into a drawer on a table by the door. He produced a laser pistol from it, its' gun metal gray color silhouetted in the dark hallway. "Just in case", Gottman commented, hefting the pistol around. "Good luck", he said shaking Jeffry's' hand. Jeffry stepped outside, looking about. Nothing! The streets were quiet. Then he heard the squall of tires on pavement. A robot police unit flashed in front of his eyes, coming to a grinding halt in front of him. "Run, boy", Gottman yelled, raising his pistol. Jeffry dived head long into some shrubbery, rolling, and then coming up in a stance.

A robot cop, its' metallic presence over shadowed by its' one gleaming infra-red eye, spoke out. "You there, halt and desist!" its metallic voice grinded out, like gears meshing in a vehicle. Gottman fired once; the ruby red flash of laser light struck the robot, almost blowing it in half! The robot on fire now, jerked madly once, and then collapsed. Jeffry Jumped then began running wildly down the street. Turning his head, he saw the robot car light up in a brilliant flash of orange light, then swing its laser cannon that was mounted on top of the vehicle, towards the old mans, house. "No", Jeffry screamed once, stopping in his tracks. He turned to see Gottman standing on the porch of his house, aiming his pistol at the robot vehicle. They both fired at the same time, engulfing the street with a panorama of orange reddish light, lighting up the sky, like fireworks.

House and human exploded, sending shards and remnants of metal and flesh everywhere. As the robot car was struck simultaneously it exploded into, a fiery fireball, cascading down the empty street. People peered out their windows in shock, afraid to venture out. Jeffry shocked by the carnage, ran home in the dark dodging into bushes along the way, whenever he saw a robot patrol coming his way. Stealthily, he crept back into the house. All was quiet! Everyone must be asleep. Perhaps the school had neglected to call his parents about today's incident. A why should they? It would make no difference to them! Tomorrow was his Death day! He returned to his room, where he collapsed on his bed in a mixture of shock, and exhaustion, awaiting the day. Jeffry awoke that morning, still exhausted from the night before.

Shaking his head, he had to clear it, if he wanted to escape his death! Getting up from bed, he went to his dresser to get a change of clothes. The ones he had slept in looked wrinkled, like a piece of cellophane that had been waded up. Getting dressed, he reached under his mattress, producing the scrambler from it. He examined it closely. Pressing the second hand of the device, he heard a sharp…click, then nothing!

"Damn it doesn't work ", he said to himself. Then he heard a curse downstairs. Stowing the scrambler away, he rushed downstairs to see what was going on. His father sat on the couch, cursing at the blank screen of the video box. "Goddamn machine", his father swore, staring at it.

Jeffry smiled, and then returned to his room to get the scrambler. It worked! Or it worked on the vid screen. Hopefully; it will work on the death day devices. His life depended on it! Jeffry snapped the bracelet that held the device to his wrist. Jeffry returned to the stairs, and then walked slowly to the breakfast table. He sat quietly at the table, while his parents discussed small matters, avoiding the events of death day that would appear all too soon. Even his sister sat quietly, not picking on him as usual. The silence then, filled the air with tension. It was so thick you could cut it with a blade. They all finished their meal quietly, and then prepared to leave the house. His parents were to drive him to the death day center at ten o'clock. Lindy, his sister balked. "No, I won't", she refused, crying. Then she did something he hadn't done in years. She reached up to Jeffry, and kissed him on the cheek. Jeffry looked in amazement! "Good…bye, Jeffry", she said haltingly, then turned and ran back into the house, slamming the door. His mother made a motion towards the house, as if to retrieve Lindy. His father gripped her arm tightly, "No", he spoke evenly, "Let her go, it's better that way". The three left, Jeffry's father driving for miles outside the city limits. Then they gazed upon it! The death day arena! It once held a crowd of spectators who came here to cheer on non lethal types of entertainment. Now it hosted the death shrouds of many a poor soul who wished to end their miserable existence.

As they entered the arena, Jeffry could see a never ending row upon row of people sitting in the bleachers. Why there must be thousands today! He stared at awe in the crowd. "We have to go now, Jeffry", his father spoke. And robot attendant approached them. "Are you the selected one? It asked, its voice sounding shrill. Jeffry shivered, "Yes I am". The robot gripped his arm firmly, but gently. Probably. Thinking I'll freak out, Jeffry thought, smiling at the machine. "Well son...' his father began, and then he turned away quickly, to keep from crying.

His mother however, flooded her face with tears, and hugged him closer to her. "Oh, Jeffry, what can I say", she wailed. Jeffry hugged her back. "Maybe I'm going to a better place, mom", he said, trying not to cry. She gave him a strange look. The robot gripped his arm tighter! "This way", it intoned, "They are waiting". Jeffry and his mother parted, as the robot tugged him along. "Hey ease up oil breath Jeffry muttered to the machine. It paused for a moment, as if contemplating the retort, and then shrugged, almost like a human, thinking better of it. The robot escorted him to the center of the arena, where the announcer in his typical loud jacket, and a referee in the traditional blue and white tunic, awaited him. The announcer stepped up to Jeffry, microphone hooked in to his respirator mask. "Must be a real important day for your son", he remarked, flashing a phony smile. Jeffry returned the phony smile of his own, thinking; "I'd like to rip that mike right out of your mask"! Jeffry continued his smile, as the referee stood close to him. A mike hooked into his mask. The referee raised his hands, to quiet the fidgeting crowd. "Please", he spoke. The crowd quelled down.

"Your attention, please", he started, the crowd sat quietly listening. He continued "for the weekly games, he paused briefly, Jeffry Coffy, a local boy, who will be a participant". Jeffry's ears rang out, as the crowd roared in response. "I will go over the rules and setup, for the contestant', the ref stated. He turned to Jeffry. Jeffry observed the man closely. It was the man whom he met in the alley! Jeffry almost spoke up, but the man shook his head. He turned his mike down to its lowest level, and then spoke quietly to Jeffry. "They 'all be waiting on the other side of the wall for you", he whispered, winking at Jeffry. Jeffry regained his composure. The referee turned up his mike. He continued his monologue. "The contestant will attempt to negotiate three laser beam walls, the beams being three feet off the ground. "He must work his way over, or under the beam, and reach the other side of the arena. Where... he paused, he may terminate himself by pressing the switch on the far wall, here he pointed, "Dying a glorious death painlessly". "However, he went on, "If the person tries to abort the game early, a robot stationed at the west wall, will roast the contestant slowly, with a laser pistol". He pointed to the robot, standing near the laser wall, its' infra red eyes scoping out the course way. Jeffry gulped. He sucked in a quick breath' "Are you ready"? The ref asked. Jeffry puffed out a blast of air, and then nodded. 'Then...begin", the ref shouted, "And good luck!" Jeffry ran towards the first wall, the crowd cheering on. He reached out, pushing the stem on the scrambler. The laser beam went dead, as he scrambled towards the second. He dashed on, knowing that somehow, real goddamn quick, they were going to catch on, and he better move his ass a little faster. He pressed the stem again, slid on his butt, then crawled under the second beam.

The crowd went crazy, egging Jeffry on. They stamped their feet, and applauded. Jeffry grinned. One more to go! He bounced up running. As he closed in on the final wall, he could see...Damn! The last one was set one foot shorter than the rest. His momentum carried him closer... to death! He threw himself down as low as he could get, eating dirt all the way under. A flash of pain erupted through his left shoulder. It had sliced a good piece out of it. He could smell the sweet, sickly odor of his burnt flesh. No time for pain! Struggling up, he stumbled towards the exit wall. The robot reacted, getting a signal from the stand, that all was not well! Jeffry was only ten yards from the wall. The robot swung and peditated, aiming its' deadly beam square at his head. Jeffry hit the stem of the scrambler. Nothing! Cursing, he threw a high curve with the device, striking the robot above its' shoulders. And explosion erupted from the robot, scattering pieces around the arena. The robotic arm, on impulse, pulled the trigger to the laser pistol. The aim was crooked, and varied, as the robot arm jerked in circles, its directional devices destroyed, spraying the field with its' deadly beam. One beam shot close to the referee. "Shit! he exclaimed, as he hit the ground rolling away.

The announcer, his respirator hanging loose with surprise, gaped open as the beam struck him, dispersing his mass upon several gawking spectators in the stands. The referee looked up looked up at Jeffry, and then shouted, "Push the button on the wall! "Push it! It's rigged". Jeffry raced to the button, and then pushed it, closing his eyes, praying he didn't explode! A section of the wall opened up, revealing the country side apart from the arena. As he raced through the opening, he turned and shouted, extending his middle finger in the old Yankee salute "Fuck you, and have a happy death day". He stumbled into the arms of several people, who had been waiting for him. "Welcome to the real world, kid", the man said, holding Jeffry up. "It's time to live again". Jeffry gazed at the people. All of them just like him! Four men and two women. One of them was about his age! Jeffry smiled. "Yes, we would like you to get to know her", the man said. "You're the only normal one who can successfully procreate." "All the others are sterile". "Only you and Darla there can make the difference". Jeffry stared at the girl. She was a pretty blonde haired girl about his age. She was short, about five feet tall, with the ruby red lips he had ever seen. He could almost taste them! "Let me introduce you two to each other." Jeffry walked over to her. "Adam, meet your Eve", the man stated, grinning wide now. Jeffry stood in awe at the girl, as she timidly took his hand. Smiling, they both stared into each other's eyes, waiting expectantly.

Chapter II

END OF FREEWAY

Thompson Boyd drove slowly down the desert highway, searching for the broken phone lines he was suppose to repair. The blazing heat of the sun beat unmercifully upon the man, as the only sound he heard was the clickety-click of the trucks tires on the broken pavement of the asphalt road. And occasional bird flew by low, as it circled the truck several times. Boyd frowned at the bird, as he reached into his back trouser pocket, producing a tattered red handkerchief, wiping sweat from his forehead. He mumbled, "Damn line must be out there somewhere". His eyes squinted in the glare. "Good thing I'm retiring this week", he said. "At 55, I'm getting to old for this shit". This made him smile. The years of working in the sun had worn his face like well tooled leather, and the years of hard drinking had made his eyes dull with the repeated bouts of drunken anger, and the rage that dwelt within. Rage, by working the same job, day after day. Long hours, and very little pay. Now was the time. After working for the phone company in Newbury Springs for thirty years, he had saved up enough to get out of this shithole he lived in.

The day began to drag on. Finally he spied the broken line. It hung there, like a victim that was waiting for the final blow. Boyd sighed, and then pulled the truck over to the side of the road, then parked it. He began to unload his gear from the back of the truck. "Damn sure wished I had a cold beer", he said to himself grunting as he bent to pick up his climbing shoes. "Being hung-over didn't help much", he thought. With a pull, he looped his climber's belt around the pole, and ascended. Groaning in pain, he climbed slowly up, till he reached the top of the pole. Pausing, he inspected the line. "Splicing it together would be a bitch", he said to no one, but himself. He thought again, "It's going to take all day". It was almost 10 a.m. now! If he was lucky, he might get done by dark.

The place that was the line was down, near the end of the freeway, was far away from anyone within twenty miles. Boyd worked on through the day, not stopping to take a break. It was getting dusk, when he finished. Using his portable phone, he tapped into the line to test it. Listening closely, he heard the wind rustling mournfully through the line. Then... Something! Or someone! There was a strange noise coming across through the phone line! Someone was listening on the other end! "Anyone there? No answer! "Hello", he repeated. Nothing! Just the strange feeling that someone was listening in. All he heard was the wind blowing through the line. It seemed to whisper ...only the dead". A chill welled up inside him. Then he shook his head to clear his morbid thoughts. "Too much to drink last night", he commented to himself. It was getting darker now. Well fuck it", he growled into the phone, then haltingly disconnected it. It could wait till tomorrow.

He began to climb down the pole, when he heard a flapping noise floating through the air above him. Looking up, a flock of crows flew close to him, almost knocking him down. "Shit!" he hollered, as he began to slide down the pole even faster, almost skinning his hands on the wooden post. Reaching the ground, he unsnapped his belt, and hopped into the truck, his climbing shoes still on his feet. "I'm out of here", he thought frantically, as he fired up the truck.

As he began to swing the truck around, a deer bounced out in front of him. Boyd slammed on his brakes, hitting his head on the dash, then all was dark. Time passed. As he came to, he shook his head slowly. Attempting to rise up, he discovered he couldn't move! He was tied up! His hands were bound securely with sharp rose vines! They were so tight his arms bled a little, when he strained against them. Looking down, he could see his legs were bound the same way. He began bucking wildly, causing the rose thistles to dig even deeper into his flesh! Boyd screamed in pain. "Shut up you"!, boomed a growling voice from the darkness. Boyd peered out in to the dark, trying to make out where the voice came from. Out of the darkness, an immense brown bear ambled towards him.

The man struggled wildly in his captivity. "Help! Help! He cried out frantically. "Shut up, human", the bear commanded, growling at him again. Boyd was thunderstruck! "You...you, speak", he stuttered. "Of course I did, idiot", retorted the bear, glaring at him. Boyd heard a rustle in the brush behind the bear. Out of the bushes came a procession of creatures.

They were creeping slowly towards him. Boyd shivered in fear. There was a deer, an owl, a wolf, skunk, and a pigeon, which flew circles around his head. They gathered around him in a large semi-circle. The wolf, its' red eyes glowing like two hot coals, reared its furry head back, and howled menacingly at the man. The hair on Boyd's' neck stood up. He stared at the animals incuriously. Regaining his speech, he asked, "Why are you holding me?" "Let's kill him now, growled the wolf, licking his lip "Quiet! commanded the bear, "Not now". The bear turned towards Boyd. "We have to wait until the big boss comes, or she'll be pissed." Who...Who was that? Boyd stuttered. "Never mind", the growled the wolf, licking his fangs again. "Let's get on with it". The wolf paced restlessly, and continued, I want his genitals for dinner, and I'm getting hungry". Boyd mentally shrank back from the wolf. "Let's wait for mother", cooed the pigeon, resting on Boyd's' head. Boyd felt something sticky running on top of his head. "Oops, sorry", said the pigeon, fluttering away to avoid the humans' wrath. "Perhaps your right little one", the bear acknowledged" We'll wait for mother, and then maybe we can all share the human…after she's done with him". The wolf frowned. "Soon, my carnivorous one", the bear soothed, soon". "We'll wait for mother", the wolf sighed, resigned. The wind picked up from nowhere, then…and oppressing odor of …something fearful filled Boyd's' nostrils.

A flash of light cascaded directly in front of him, followed by a whirlwind that shimmered, changing into a definite shape. The shape of …a woman! But a very unusual one. There she stood, her raven black hair, flowing freely, cascading down her shoulders, and passed her spine. She wore a see through flimsy night dress. Her nipples stood fair and proud through the garment. Her eyes twinkled emerald green, with a trace of hostility, projecting. "Who the hell are you? Boyd stated, highly irate now at being trussed up like a Christmas tree ornament. "Silence human", she hissed, waving an arm at him. Boyd swallowed, but could not speak. He had lost his voice! The woman continued, "you will listen an attend to what I will tell you! Boyd's' eyes bulged from his sockets in anger, but nodded his head weakly, unable to speak. The woman smiled now, gliding...Yes, gliding closer to him! "I am an elemental spirit, and have existed though the millennium of time". I am the protector of all nature and its creatures". She paused. Then went on "I am the one you humans call...Mother Nature! She rambled on, Boyd being a captive audience. "We declare war on you humans!" "The beings of the forest and I grew weary of your disregard for the earth, and its' environment. Unfortunately, the great spirit of us all...or shall I say blessed me, hear she paused to gaze into the sky. She went on... With this curious urge to make love with a human, which occurs every 200 years or so! Boyd's, eyes grew larger. "Yes, she said, "you are the chosen one". She turned to the bear and commented, "Not much to look at is he?" The bear shrugged, "all we could find that was alone"< he replied, "The town drunk". "No one will miss this one". Sad but true, Boyd thought. He never was much of a socializer, anyway. Her voice grew gentler. "The feelings, the hormonal surge of human lust, is beginning to well up deep within me" she whispered, hoarsely, removing her night dress, revealing the human, and most impressive naked female Boyd had ever seen". Boyd felt, almost emotionally erect! "You may speak now! she commanded him. She cooed, like a bird, rubbing her soft white hands along her body, sighing with every stroke. Boyd swallowed hard. No way was he in the mood for this! Especially with a supernatural being who was going to let those damn animals have him for kibble later. Gathering strength, he replied "I can't now, maybe if you untied me first".

Her eyes glared a Kelly green, as lightning bolts struck near him, almost blinding his eyes! "Maybe", she said coolly, "If not, it's not nice to turn down Mother Nature!" With a swift gesture, she pointed towards her dazzling naked body. Animals appeared, projecting from it like a nightmarish three-d hologram. They bellowed and roared, scratched and clawed in the air, then vanished quickly as they had come. Boyd shuddered at the apparitions. No way now, would he let that creature close to his skin! She said, "You have 30 of your human minutes to decide your fate". With that, she walked away towards the brush, as all the animals followed her, except for the brown bear. The bear reached out and snagged a cigar from Boyd's' pocket, and a book of matches. He lit the cigar deftly.

The bear puffed on it, until the tip glowed red. Then he blew a couple of smoke rings into Boyd's' face. It gave out a guttural laugh, "think it over chum. The time with her will make your time with us feel like heaven". The bear coughed, and then gagged on the cigar. "Damn, these are bad for you". The bear gingerly put out the cigar carefully on the ground, still coughing. "Hope you choke turkey"< Boyd laughed. The bear growled. He tore the matches in shreds with his claws, and then flung them violently into Boyd's face. "Only you can prevent fires", the bear cackled, looping off to join the others. Boyd hung his head in despair. What to do? Any time they would be back. A sound fluttered near his ears. The pigeon! Boyd flinched, expecting another onslaught to the dried mess already formed in his hair. Instead it whispered in his ear. "I'll free you if you promise to tell no one of your experience". Boyd did not hesitate, but nodded emphatically. "You must never tell a single soul", it twittered, loosening the thistles from his hands with it's' beak.

Boyd just stared at the bird. "We pigeons are non-violent. "We're messengers, not assassins". The tone in its voice changed for a moment. "However, it warned, if you tell, there are many of us, and we will find you". As the remaining bonds were severed, Boyd ran like hell. "I'll keep them busy", the bird chirped, then flew back to the others. As Boyd dashed through the woods, he heard the pigeons parting speech. "Mother nature will return to a spirit shortly, and will not be able to get you!" Boyd didn't wait around to find out. He ran quickly through the briars and the bramble, looking for his truck. Meanwhile, the pigeon flew over the group, depositing amounts of its excrement on a few. "Oops! OopS!" it quipped, as several creatures wre bombarded, including Mother Nature. "I always do that when I get excited!" The bird shrilled, the human ...was getting away". The creatures roared to life. Mother Nature cried out in frustration, Get him! Bring him to me! "I don't have much time left". The animals scurried off through the brush, in hot pursuit. Boyd heard the commotion, and pumped his legs faster, his heart racing loudly. He ran blindly for five miles! Then he saw it! He knew the animals couldn't have carried him too far. The end of freeway sign, and his truck!

Gathering up his last vestiges of energy, he raced to the truck, and safety. Collapsing into the seat, he found his keys, still in the ignition. Fumbling, he started the motor. Turning the truck around, his headlights fell upon the shape of the wolf, glaring at him. "Eat this!", hollered the man, as he gunned his truck, striking the wolf with a glancing blow, landing with a thud! The wolf went hurtling into the bush, lifeless. Boyd revved the motor, and raced down the desert road. A flash of light appeared in front of him. The image of Mother Nature! Not so glamorous this time though! She stood in the road, a vision of hatred! Her arms outstretched, the animals howling from her skin, her eyes reflected a ghastly, even putrid luminescent putrid green. She spoke, "You have won this round, human!" Then a sinister smile formed on her lips, "till next time". "Screw that!", Boyd shouted, shifting into high, passing through the image of Mother Nature, who laughed manically, then transformed into a whirlwind, shattering the trucks windows.

Bleeding slightly, Boyd kept going at high speed, never stopping, until he got to town. Boyd said nothing of his ordeal to no one, keeping his promise. He retired the following day, early, and moved to Los Angeles, where he felt safer. The more crowded around people the better. When a flock of birds flew over him, or a lightning storm gathered, he panicked, and ran to the nearest shelter. People laughed at him, thinking he was drunk, or senile, or both. But Boyd knew better. He was keeping his promise! Sometimes at night, the phone would ring. Picking it up, he heard nothing on the line! Just wind! Then he would hang up, his face pale with fear. Returning to his bed, he grabbed his bottle of bourbon off the night stand, and downed it. He drifted off to sleep, he hoped to avoid the demons of the night.

Chapter III

I AM MONSTER!

The water was deep, and murky. The body of a man rested upon the bottom, gathering murky mud and weeds around it. The body lay motionless, surrounded in a collection of flesh and bone. A fish swam by, and began to nibble around the fleshy parts of the eye. The eyes flew open! I became aware! The fish swam away, frightened by the movement. I sat up in the water, my vision somewhat blurred. I rose up, looking about. Water! I slowly moved to shore. Stepping on dry land, I gazed, blinking my eyes at my surroundings. "My legs? Started to buckle. Reaching out, I grasped the Thornberry bush with my left hand. I stood, balancing myself. Gazing at my left hand, I noticed several thorns from the bush imbedded in my hand. Hoe curious, no feelings of pain! I continued on, noticing the sun about to set. Who am I? Where am I? These questions remained unanswered to me. By some instinct, I moved slowly down a well worn path of mildewed grass, and rocks.

Some instinct was pulling me along an unknown direction. Plodding along, I could hear the sounds of my decrepit body. Squish! Pop! Squish pop! My joints began to loosen up, and I gained flexibility. Heading west, I think, to somewhere! The stars were out now, gleaming down the dark path. I heard a rustling in the bushes! A coyote appeared, on a direct path to me. I stopped, frozen in fear! The coyote, a huge grey monster, approached me sniffing. The coyote stopped, staring at me. It howled, than it began a low, deep, growling sound. I growled back at it, stepping towards it. It yelped a few times, turned tail, and ran away. Maybe I'm scared it more than I was. I continued plodding along. The night air was warm, but I felt little of it. Then I saw it! A huge house, practically a mansion, a hundred yards away.

The lights burned brightly, as I approached it. I stepped up onto the porch, slowly. A dog appeared. It looked like and Australian Shepherd. White fur, with a black circle around its right eye. I stopped hesitating to move. It approached me, sniffing cautiously. I stood perfectly still. Then surprisingly, the dog sat down, wagging its' tail. Memories flashed through me! I had played Frisbee…with Lucy! That was her name. She was my dog! I bent down to pet her, as she wagged her tail back and forth. "Good girl", I said, my voice sounding like sandpaper rubbing against metal.

She cocked her head, giving me a curious look. "Shh!' I said, in a low even voice. I started up further on the porch. A light transcended from a window, illuminating a part of the inside. I crept up to the window. Peering inside, there sitting on a couch, were a man and a woman. The man about thirty-five years of age sat on the couch in his underwear. The woman, a striking blonde about the same age, was sitting next to him in her white nighty, it clinging to her athletic frame. Wow! No panties! I could just make out the fluff of her pubic hair.

The memories of these two flooded my brain. I knew them! The woman was my wife Dora, and the man was my lawyer, Bill. Flashes of memories blazed through me, like a spreading fire! I was having a drink with Dora, when everything went dark. The next thing I knew, I woke up at the bottom of the lake! They were both laughing now. I could hardly make out the voices. "It's done, and we'll be rich"< Dora laughed, fondly Bills' private parts through his underwear. A sudden heat came across my face. My hands were clenched in fists of anger! Then I spied my reflection in the window! A half eaten corpse, wrapped in mud and weeds! My wife and lawyer had plotted to get control of my fortune! Dora must have slipped some poison in my drink. Her and Bill had deposited, my body in the lake. I reached down and petted Lucy, my lone companion. I stared at the couple on the couch. They will get a surprise from me soon!

FOR I AM MONSTER AND I WILL AVENGE!

Chapter IV

THE INCUBUS

The Incubus floated among the billowy clouds, a fine mist, making it almost invisible to the naked eye. It had been a while between feedings. It fed on the unfulfilled desires of the human female. Its' sense of this drew it nearer to its prey. Circling and old barn, it spied a woman lying in a hay loft, eating an apple. Half asleep, her long dark hair cascaded among the golden strands of alfalfa. The Incubus came lower, smelling her lustful desires that were hidden. A virgin, it smelled, ripe for the picking! It descended down upon her. Then it attacked! It entered her body and mind swiftly. She convulsed, her senses filled with wave after wave of physical and mental orgasms. She thrashed violently around. The Incubus settled in. Sitting up, mesmerized, she climbed down the ladder from the loft. Walking as if in a trance, she crossed the yard to where the firewood lay stacked in a neat pile. The sharpened axe lying next to it. She ripped her dress and undergarments from her body. Smiling widely now, she picked up the axe. Lizzy headed towards the front door of her house, to greet her parents! **FREE AT LAST!**

Chapter V

SISSY!

Hey Sissy! The words rang out in Billy's' ears. Billy
ran as fast as his legs could go. He hiked his dress up, so he
could acquire more speed. The two bullies, Ed and Fred, were
almost upon him. Billy saw the white picket fence of his house.
He vaulted over it, in one leaping bound. The two bullies
stopped, then took off in another direction. Billy huffing ran
into the house. His mom, standing there, her long red hair
flowing, wrapped in a kitchen apron, gazed at him. "What's
wrong with you girl", she asked. Billy replied, "Same old crap,

mom". "It's not lady like to say crap, "his mom stated. "I'm not a lady", Billy retorted, knowing what his mother would say. "Wilma, go to your room", she said harshly. Reluctantly, he headed up the stairs to his room.

The room was a pasty pink, with fluffy curtains. Everything was feminine in the room, from the Hello Kitty bed sheets to the nicely framed mirror with dress ads, taped to it. He stripped off his dress, bra, and panties. He lay down on his bed, but first made sure the bedroom door was closed, and locked. Reaching under the mattress, he took out a Playboy magazine. "I'm a boy, not a girl", he said to himself. He thumbed through the magazine, till he came to the centerfold. A blonde, with big boobs, her pubic area peeking out. "I have a penis, not a vagina", he said to himself, gazing at the centerfold. He began massaging his penis. After he had climaxed, he went into the bathroom, and showered. Drying off, he slipped into a pair of pink shorts, panties, and a Hello Kitty t shirt. He hated wearing this stuff. He wished his mom would get it together. When his father left, just before Billy was born, his mother swore off men for life. Maybe that was why Billy had been born with a girls' name, Wilma. He had born the insults of it far too; long. At school, the kids teased him, and the two bullies were the instigators.' His only friend, Jenny, was fifteen, the same age as him. She didn't care what he was. They had played together since they were five years old. The only problem was when she hugged him, Billy had noticed her emerging breasts, and started to feel something hard between his legs. "I'm a boy", he said harshly.

The phone rang downstairs. His mom answered it. She was yelling into the phone with someone. Then, she slammed the receiver down. "Wilma, "she called him from the bottom of the stairs. "What is it, mom? He asked, descending the stairs. She stood rigidly, her face purple with rage. "Those goddamn school people want to remove you from school!" "Why? He asked, but he knew the answer. "Those bastards, she replied, want you to attend a special, more advanced school!' "You have none", she finished. "To hell with them", Billy retorted. Billy and his mother sat down for dinner. "I can't use the restroom at school, he stated, I have to use the one in the teachers' lounge". His mother muttered curses under her breath. "You stay home from school, tomorrow", she stated flatly, "Until I talk to the principal." O.K., "Billy said smiling.

He helped mom with the dishes. Then they sat down on the couch to watch TV. The phone rang, and Billy got up to answer it. It was Jenny! "Hi there", she spoke softly. "Can you meet me in the park, about ten"? "Sure", he said. Jenny continued, "I know you're a boy, she whispered softly, "I want us to be girlfriend, and boyfriend". "Alright", he said, "Meet you at ten". He hung up the phone. He had to wait till his mom went to bed. She always went at nine thirty. She got up to go to bed. "Goodnight, honey", she yawned, giving him a kiss on the cheek. "Goodnight mom", he replied, waiting for her to go to sleep. Billy went up stairs to his room. He had hidden some male clothes under his bed, which Jenny had got from her older brother. Blue jeans and a t-shirt, with ACDC on it. He quickly dressed, and sneaked out through his bedroom window. He made his way down a long path, to the park. Jenny was waiting for him, dressed in a tank top, and Daisy Duke shorts. She hugged him. He felt the arousal from between his legs. "I love you, Billy", she whispered in his ear. Then they kissed, timidly at first. Billy touched her breasts. "Yes", she moaned, encouraging him.

She reached down between his legs, and gently squeezed. He felt himself getting hard. They lay down on the grass, fumbling with their clothes. Billy entered her. She gasped, and then wrapped her legs tightly around him. When they had finished, they lay there catching their breath. "I love you Billy", she said softly. "I love you too", he replied. Suddenly, he felt rough hands grabbing him! It was those two assholes, Ed and Fred! "A fagot like you shouldn't have sex with a girl, Ed said, kicking Billy in the crotch. "Run Jen", Billy gasped, through the pain. Jenny grabbed her clothes, putting them on as she ran. "I'll get dad", she hollered back at him. The two bullies kept pounding Billy with their hands and feet. Billy almost passed out. 'You want to be a girl, fagot", Fred said. "Then we'll treat you like one." Held Billy down, as Ed straddled Billy fought them, but was no match for the two. They were bigger and heavier than him. Billy was held spread eagled on the ground. He heard Ends' zipper go down. Billy hollered, but Ed entered him, sodomizing him till Ed shuddered in climax. "Your turn Fred", Ed said, zipping up his trousers. Fred replied, "I'd rather cut off his privates, and make him a girl". Fred produced a large, sharp butchers' knife, about eight inches long. Billy's' mind screamed. "This can't be happening! "I'm a boy! Billy screamed out, pulling himself up, his adrenaline pulsing to its fullest potential.

Jenny ran home, to get her dad. She left out the part about sex, but told him everything else. Her dad got dressed, pulling out his twenty two revolvers from his desk. They then left. Meanwhile, his mom woke up, hearing Billy come in. "What the hell is going on? She asked. Billy sat on the floor, covered in blood. She looked at Billy, startled. "My God girl, she spoke, what did they do to you? Billy sat sprawled, holding something in his hands. She switched on the hall light. There was something bloody in his hands! She squinted in the light, then almost screamed. "I'm a boy, mom", he yelled. "Now these bullies are the sissies! He held up two sets of male genitals in his hands. His moms' mind reeled at the sight, and then passed out from the horror of it all. Billy just smiled, widely.

Chapter VI

SWEET OCTOBER

Her Lithe naked body crossed the room, padding quietly towards the full length mirror installed in the closet door. She looked herself over. Her hands moved slowly over her body. She examined her breasts, pert and firm. Her hands drifted down to the dark curly hair of her pubic area. She brushed the area lightly with her hands. Perfect! Her hands traveled down her smooth golden legs. Yes! She was of Asian descent! Her mellow dark eyes, almost black, gazed in the mirror.

So young, she thought, never to have a life of her own. Since her birth, she had always lived in the mansion. A beautiful cage, but still a cage. She had no knowledge of her parents. The Master was one of the few she had known. One of the others, Chris, always friendly, but still her shadow! Her security guard. Now she had learned why she was here. Her eighteenth birthday, October thirty first, was here! There was to be a feast in her honor, and she was the main course! Raised on organic food, so there would be no impurities in her system. She had cried at first, and then came depression, and finally she became resigned to it. She had attempted to escape twice. The gates were all secured, and electrified. Chris always came to get her. She saw reluctance in his eyes. She knew he felt something for her, but was afraid to say so, because of the Master. She had heard the master threaten Chris, about his mother and sister.

Chris, at six feet tall, and two hundred pounds, with those sparkling blue eyes! His eyes twinkled a little bit, when he talked to her. He towered above her slim, five foot tall, ninety pounds of her. When he touched her, she fantasized about having sex with him. She had masturbated in her room, feeling a sense of release, but left her unfulfilled. Now today, there may be no chance of that. Today would be her last! But she had a plan, hoping it would work. She would talk Chris into having sex with her. Then she could persuade him to help her. She hoped she could get the Masters' keys to the lab. She hoped it could work. She slipped into her terry cloth robe, and her pink flip flops.

She left the room, and descended down the long mahogany staircase, glancing at the paintings on the wall. Rembrandt, Picasso, all original. No object the Master couldn't obtain. Including her! At the bottom of the stairs, Chris stood, waiting for her. "How are you beautiful", he asked. "Just fine, handsome", she smiled sexily. She reached the bottom of the stairs, letting her robe open slightly, revealing her assets. Chris stared at her greedily, his mouth open in surprise. She reached down, and touched his crotch, briefly. Then she took his hand. "The library", she whispered softly. They walked together through the large oak doors of the library. She dropped her robe, and lay down on the soft leather couch there. "They wanted a virgin," she said softly, "Take it away from them! She opened up for him. Chris disrobed, and then he entered her quickly. She felt a sharp pain, and then relaxed. They began moving in rhythm with each movement. They climaxed, both gasping from the exertion. "I need to clean up, lover", she said, getting up. She entered the plush bathroom just to the left of them. She grabbed some soap, and then entered the shower. The warm spray of water made her feel better. Getting out, she dried herself. Coming out, she saw Chris getting dressed. "I need your help, honey", she stated flatly. "How? He asked." I need to get the lab keys, "To get revenge on the Master". "I can do that, he said, "Anything for you! Chris reached in his pocket, and produced a set of keys."I need to find a poison", she remarked. Chris gazed at her sadly, but nodded. She took the keys; she left the library, going two doors down to the great metal doors of the lab. She unlocked them, and then entered. She looked at the rows of vials and beakers. Many texts and volumes of books sat on a shelf. Then, she found what she wanted. She wanted a poison that would not dissipate from cold and heat, and would absorb itself through blood and skin.

She matched the ingredients from the text, to one of the vials. "I'm going to poison those bastards" she said. "After I'm gone". She smiled viciously, to herself, mixing the poison.

She left the library, and saw Chris outside the door, waiting for her. "I'm going to poison those bastards", she repeated to him. Chris gave her a startled look, and gripped her hand. "It's ok", she said softly, "for both of us". "After I'm gone, burn this evil place to the ground". He nodded his head slowly. She left him there, his head hanging low. She knew he would do it! She drifted up stairs, to her bedroom. "Now all I do is wait", she said to herself. They were going to give her and injection of Potassium Chlorate, to stop her heart. Not that it was a kindness of the Master. It was so they wouldn't hear her screams. She heard several sets of footsteps, coming up the stairs. It was Time! She drank the poison quickly. *Bon Appetite, you freaks!*

Chapter VII

SHAPE SHIFTER

The coyote sat waiting along the desert highway. Waiting! But for what? sitting there puzzled. Why did he do this? He should be out hunting game. His female would be angry if he didn't come back with something to eat. He gave a snort, and then took off to look for food. Miles Bannon drove slowly down the highway, searching. He was a man obsessed with one thing only. To find his brother Paul, who had turned up missing two weeks ago? Paul had come out to the desert to study the wild life there. He had received a grant from college to study the wild life out there. He had received the grant for the summer for his masters 'thesis. A report of finding his truck in the desert was given to him by the highway patrol. The truck had been found near Needles, on the old highway 66. No signs of struggle or violence, except Paul's' shredded clothing. The clothing had been found near the truck. Miles felt that the CHP hadn't looked hard enough for Paul they had figured he had simply gotten heat stroke, wandered off, and died from lack of water. The search area revealed nothing! No body or bleached bones from the sun and the wind. Miles refused to give up. Somewhere, Paul was out there, and alive or dead, he would find him.

Miles drove on, searching the desert road. The coyote arrived at the cave exhausted. His female glared at him. He had found one old tattered rabbit, to slow to run, and killed it. Bringing his prize in, he lay the rabbit at his mates' feet. The female sniffed contemptuously at the dead animal, then began to devour part of it. The male waited until she was done, and then helped himself to the remainder of it. Satisfied they both lay down. They curled up together, to keep themselves warm. The male fell asleep, and began to dream. The same face kept recurring in his dreams. A human face! He was calling the coyote by some strange sounding name. "Paul, are you alright, Paul? The coyote thrashed in his sleep. The female alarmed, moved to the other side of the cave. She tried again to sleep. The male awoke, and gazed out the cave. Sunlight! He dashed out the cave, heading for the highway.

The female awoke, and slipped out the cave, to follow the male. The male dashed down the road, his heart leaping! He now knew the reason he waited at the highway every day! At one time he had been a human, named Paul. He had been bitten by the female, and it had transformed him to a coyote. The female was a shape shifter. The only one of her breed that existed on this earth! NEEDING a mate, she had come across Paul, and had nipped his right hand. The change had been so dramatic, it cost him his memory of being human. The man in his dreams was his brother, Miles! He must find him. Maybe he could help him somehow.

The male raced down the road, unaware that the female was following behind. Miles drove quickly down the road, heading were the truck was found. The male skidded into the highway, not able to stop because of his gain of speed. Miles came around the bend in the road. The coyote was sitting in the middle of the road. Miles braked hard, it was too late! The car struck the coyote head on, sending the animal flying through the air. It landed in a ditch on the opposite side of the road. Miles, shook up, got out of the vehicle, and rushed over to the animal. Looking down, miles shook his head in disbelief. The coyote began to squirm, changing shape, into a man! Miles stunned, bent down to see his brother. Laying there, a pool of blood dripping from his mouth, his limbs broken on impact. "Oh my God", he cried clutching his brother. A gust of dusty sand blew crazily around him. Looking up in the dust, he observed a naked woman standing in the road. Long dark hair covered her breasts, and pubic area. She appeared to be Native American. Stunned by the whole scene, he watched as she approached him, and then leaped up, biting his shoulder. She mourned her mate, but was realistic. She needed another male to help her. Pups will be born soon. She stepped back a few feet, and waited. Miles sat in shock, his mind slowly drifting away. The female waited patiently for the change!

Chapter VIII

WHEN THE RAINS COME

The rain poured down in torrents. What had once been a busy boulevard, now a giant lake? Nothing could be seen. Cars had fell prey to the continued pouring, as did many people, sinking below the surfaces of the street. Nothing was spared! The water had risen up to twenty five feet already. It had drowned out the stores, and apartment buildings. This had gone on for thirty days. Now, without stopping. Jerry Marsh stood at his window, on the thirty fifth floors, gazing down upon the watery scene. Thirty days, he thought to himself, and no stopping or letting up. Jerry gave a small sigh, and then left the window. He looked around his small studio apartment a couch that turned into a bed, the small kitchenette he couldn't use. Power had gone out awhile back.

Jerry found several candles in a small drawer in the kitchen, and some wooden matches. The candles and matches were short lived alone and in the dark, soon. The rain kept pounding on the window sill. There has to be a way out, somehow, he thought. Soon, the water would be up to thirty five feet, and he would be screwed! The only escape was to get up on the roof! Jerry paced the floor. Jerry started to form a plan. In the mean time, jerry listened on his short wave radio.

The batteries were almost gone. The news cast stated the moon had shifted out of orbit, causing major changes around the world. High tides, low tides. The people in San Francisco had surfed to Denver!, Australia had been hit by a giant tsunami. It had totally wiped out Perth, Melbourne, and other regions there. New York went under the rain, with the Statue of Liberty's' head peeking out of the massive waves. Her e inL.A, it was just as bad. But Jerry had found refuge in this tall apartment building. The water then, was only fifteen feet high. He had been here for three weeks, now. Three Weeks! And the water level had risen ten more feet. Jerry had come back from a canoeing trip in Colorado. He was also an expert mountain climber, having scaled some of the Rocky Mountains. His inflatable raft was tied down on top of his Humvee.

His climbing gear was in the back. The rain had risen up to his driver's window. Time to get out! He slowly opened the door. The water started rushing in. grasping the door; He was being flung against the truck. Grasping the edge of the door, he stained to reach his backpack. His hand fumbled for it, hanging on to the door with his other hand. Sweating, and straining, he retrieved it, and quickly slipped it on clumsily, because of only using his free hand. Once he slipped it on, halfway, he began swinging himself up to the roof of the hum vie. He adjusted his backpack, clinging on to the roof of his truck. Fortunately, he had been in a hurry to get back, and had not deflated the raft. The two oars were strapped to the raft. Untying the raft, he slipped into it, the rain continued to pound him relentlessly. He grabs the oars, and then pushed off the raft into the water. Struggling with the raft, upside down, he righted it up, holding on to the oars. He was water soaked to the bone. He began rowing away from the truck.

The rain continued beating on him. He heard a woman screaming. A brunette, in business attire, was swimming towards him. Jerry reached out for her. A R. V. came rushing towards her in the stream. She screamed once, and the vehicle ran over her. Helpless to help, Jerry saw no other movement in the water. He continued paddling the raft. Stores, banks, and the local police station were already under water. Jerry continued on for miles. Then he spotted a tall apartment building to the left of him. He began furiously paddling towards the building. He arrived at the main doors. Airtight, no water had entered the building. Bailing out of the raft, he pushed open the main doors. Water rushed in as he entered, then he quickly shut the doors.

Some electricity in the building was still operating, so the doors had worked, without a struggle. Jerry had entered the lobby, shaking off the cold. He needed to get up high enough in the building to avoid the rising water level. He wondered if the elevators still functioned. In answer to his question, the interior lights dimmed, like a candle in a draft, then darkness. "Damn", Jerry said, "Now what", he mumbled. There were thirty five floors in this building. How the hell was he going to get up there? Jerry started looking around the area. Remembering he kept a flashlight in his backpack, he took it off, and searched around for his light. He found his mag light, and then switched it on. He cautiously moved around the lobby, shining the light. Flashing the light, he spied the kitchen. Entering he saw several can goods on a shelf. The meat in the big walk in freezer would go bad, but the can goods could last a long time.

He loaded up his backpack as full as he could. Now, how to get up to the top floor and searched around the kitchen. Then he spotted the dumb waiter. He might be able to pull himself up to the thirty fifth floor... It was going to be strenuous, probably taking a while. Jerry opened the door to the dumb waiter, and squatted down to fit in it. A tight fit, as his backpack was loaded. If he could climb the Rocky, he could make the trip to the top floor. He started pulling up on the rope, to make his ascent. Straining, pulling, sweating profusely, he pulled as hard as he could. Pausing between floors, he remembered his climbing gloves in his backpack. His hands were cracked, and started to bleed. Holding on to the rope of the dumb waiter, with his right hand he reached into his pack. Struggling, he fumbled for his gloves, almost slipping off the rope. He found them, and then extracted them from the pack. Several food cans fell out, hitting the bottom of the shaft, making a hollow echo. "Couldn't be helped", he said to himself. Carefully slipping on his gloves, switching hands back and forth he began to pull up on the rope more. Exhausted, he finally made it to the top, and stepped out in a crouch, to survey the area. The thirty fifth floors were a luxury is, now dimmed by the darkness. Jerry started trying each apartment door. The first door, 3502, he knocked on first.

To his surprise, the door slowly creaked open. A woman stood at the opening. She looked to be in her thirties. She was very large! At about five feet tall, but must have weighed at least three hundred pounds. She spoke quietly, "Hi! My name is LULU". Jerry smiled at her. At least, he had a neighbor! Then she belched, and let go some flatulence in the air. "Oops, sorry", she apologized, her face turning red, and then slammed the door. Jerry laughed, and then went to the next door, 3504. He knocked on it. A highly nasal pitch voiced replied. "Who the fuck is it?" He continued, "If you've come to rob me, I got a surprise for you!" The door flung open, revealing a raggedy looking individual holding a 12 gauge shotgun. Jerry could smell him, and when he breathed, it smelled like cheap wine. Jerry took a step back, raising his hands. "Man I don't want any trouble", Jerry said nervously. "Who are you?" the man asked his finger still on the trigger. Jerry swallowed hard, before replying. "I just found my way up here", he said, "Looking for an empty room to stay in". "Well," the man stated, try 3506". The man looked down at Jerry's' hands, which were bleeding through the gloves. He lowered the shotgun, and glanced at Jerry's hands again. "Had to climb up the dumb waiter", jerry said. "The elevators were out". "Damn, ", the man responded, "I knew something had happened when the lights went out". "Come in", the man stated.

Jerry glanced around the apartment. Everything was in a mess! Several cases of cheap wine and scattered cans of food lay around the floor. Jerry side stepped the mess. "I have a first aid kit here", the man said, going into the bathroom. He returned with the kit. Jerry could smell the bathroom. It really stinks! But where else could the man go? Jerry shook his head. The man handed Jerry the kit as Jerry applied some ointment. The man began talking, "Been here about a week.

The rain level was was only eight feet, and the elevators were still working". He continued, "Been homeless for five years, found my way here". "I'm a Vietnam vet, but nobody gave a shit", then he coughed. Jerry listened intently. "I had a home, a wife, unfortunately, no children." We were happy! Then my wife died of breast cancer. I began drinking; using drugs, not paying my bills, and I lost the house. So fuck it, here I am! Jerry looked at the man sympathetically, and asked, "Whets your name? Jerry asked. "Just Joe", he smiled, through his rotted teeth. Jerry observed the man's' appearance.

His grey dirty beard, his long stringy hair, tattered jeans, and holey woolen shirt draped over his body was a well worn army fatigue jacket. "Who are you? Joe asked. "Jerry marsh, glad to know you". They shook hands. The man looked at Jerry in surprise. "The mountain climber? He asked. "Sure Jerry replied, how did you know? 'I saw your head line in the newspaper, and then I folded it up, and stuck it in my shoes. They were holey, so it kept me warm". Jerry laughed" At least it was good for something". Joe laughed too. "You should check the other apartments with me for supplies '. Jerry replied "Let's go". They scavenged through several apartments. They came up with two bottles of scotch, a couple cases of bottled water, and some can goods. Jerry found a forty five automatic pistol. Jerry stuffed the pistol into his waist band. "I'd better keep this", Jerry said, to Joe. Joe replied, "Whatever".

They lugged their prizes back to Joe's room. "You should take the pad at 3508, it's empty, and close by". Jerry thought, 'that's a good idea, we all need each other to survive". Jerry and Joe split up the goods. Jerry entered the apartment at 3508. It had a fold up bed that converted in to a couch. Cupboards were bare though! A microwave, whoopee! And a fridge full of rotted food. The only saving grace was the view, little as it was. Now it was two weeks later, and things were getting really, hairy! Jerry had visited Lulu, and the old man, frequently. Checking up on Lulu, she had found a bathrobe, which was too tight for her, and was naked underneath. She had lost a good twenty pounds, though. But she did look a little gaunt. Jerry tried not to notice her naked body under the robe. Lulu was stuffing her face with chocolates.

When she saw him looking at her, she stopped, and grabbed a paper towel to wipe if the dark mess. "Excuse me, "she said. She went into the bathroom, and came out fifteen minutes later. Her hair tied back in a pony tail, and had applied some make up on. It was pink, and not bad to look at her lips. Jerry looked at her empathetically; He could see she was once very attractive. "I know", she said, sitting on the hide a bed. She continued, I was very attractive three years ago. She went on, "Hear look', She handed him a magazine folded up near the bed. It was a photo shoot of an attractive blonde, clad in only a skimpy negligee. "That was me", she said, starting to tear up a little. Jerry waited for her to continue. "Three years ago, I was beaten and raped by a stalker. "It destroyed my life! She went on farther. "I became depressed, started drinking, and overeating, of course. "That way no one would want to assault me'. Here the tears began flowing more. She cried, putting her head on Jerry's' shoulder.

Anger and empathy entered his mind. "Damn bastard", Jerry thought. Jerry held her, and then decided to get up. She kissed him on his cheek. "Sorry", she said, sadly. "You have nothing to be sorry about< ", Jerry stated emphatically, "I'll come back later". "I'm going to look in on the old man. "O.K., she said, smiling at him. And she continued, "Thank you". Jerry nodded his head. He then went down the hall to Joes. Jerry knocked. Joe opened the door, staggering a bit. "You ok?" Jerry asked. "Just a little shit faced, is all", Joe replied. He grinned, a little lopsided."Come in", Joe slurred. Joe staggered to the couch. Jerry stepped in, just standing there. "What happened?, Jerry asked. "Bad dreams", again, Joe said, sinking into the couch.

Then he threw up, and urinated in his pants. "Oh, great, jerry said, "He's passed out". Jerry helped Joe out of his clothes, and covered him up as could as he could, with Joe's sleeping bag, and a blanket Jerry found in the closet. Jerry checked Joe's pulse. Steady! Then he quietly left. He knocked on Lulu's door. She answered it, still clad in the tight bathrobe. Jerry told her, "Joe's out of it, Lulu, check on him in a little while. Lulu nodded yes. Jerry returned to his apartment. He started thinking about survival. How would he get Joe and Lulu, to safety, and himself! In jerry's' backpack, he had some climbing rope, and a grappling hook attached to it. He could probably repel up to the top of the roof, then swing over to the next building, which was less covered in water. But how the hell could he get Lulu, and Joe to climb up the rope. Jerry decided to rest on the couch, and think about it.

When he awoke, he could see it was dark. Getting up, he fumbled for the candle, and the matches. Lighting a candle, he looked around. No sound! Everything was quiet! The he heard a soft knock on the door. It was Lulu. She said softly, "can I come in? Jerry opened the door. Lulu had found a way to wash her hair, and the makeup she wore looked nice. Jerry said, Wow!, come in". She staggered in drunk. The smell of cheap wine, and perfume filled the air. "Got a little tipsy from Joe's wine", she giggled. She continued, slurring a little, "He's ok, but still passed out". Lulu sat down on his couch. Jerry had noticed her ample breasts. "I think I'm in lust Jerry". She took his hand and placed it on her breasts.

Jerry gulped! He had never made love to a full figured woman before. But what the hell! Times were different. And they were just two desperate people who needed comfort. So they had sex. It was intense, but brief. They both climaxed together. Then Lulu got up. "I'm going to my apartment to clean up, Jerry", she said. "Ok, "Jerry said, putting on his clothes. Lulu left, while Jerry contemplated. "That was really good", he said. A sudden rush of footsteps filled his ears. "what the hell', Jerry said, is there somebody else hear? Then Jerry heard shouts. Lulu was screaming, and Joe was yelling! Jerry jumped to his feet, and grabbed the forty five. He raced out the door! Lulu's door was smashed open. There he saw two ragged looking men holding Lulu down. Joe was next to her, lying on his side, bleeding from his abdomen. "Fuck you sons of bitches!, Joe gasped. The one man who was holding a knife to Lulu's throat, while the other was trying to pry her legs apart. The man grunted, "Relax bitch, you'll like it". Jerry stepped in, cocking the forty five. The man with the knife jumped up. 'Get the hell out of here", he yelled, flashing the knife at Jerry. Jerry fired, two rounds hitting the man in the face, gushing blood splatter everywhere.

Lulu screamed again. The man between Lulu's legs, jumped up, covered in his buddy's' gore. "Hey wait!, the man pleaded. "Go to hell", Jerry barked, and fired again, hitting the man square in the chest. He gasped once, and fell over. Lulu ran to the back of the room, and curled up in a fetal position. Jerry stooped over Joe, bleeding immensely. "Joe", Jerry said, lifting him up to a sitting position. Joe was holding his stomach, his blood seeping through his fingers. "I'm screwed, Jerry", he gasped. "They got me in the liver". Jerry shook his head sadly. "Jerry", he said, gets me a bottle of wine, for my last drink". Jerry nodded, then rushed to Joe's room. Grabbing a bottle out of the case, jerry returned to Lulus' room. Lulu still sat quietly in the corner, staring into space.

Jerry reached Joe, now sprawled on the floor. Joes' eyes were wide open, but he wasn't breathing. "Damn, Damn this", jerry yelled, almost in tears. Jerry picked up Joes' body, and carried him to his room. There jerry placed Joe gently down on the couch. He put a bottle of wine next to him, then he covered him up, with the sleeping bag and the blanket. Jerry fired up in the air once, with the forty five. "Best military funeral I could give you, soldier", he said. He shut Joes' door,

He then returned to lulus' room. She still sat there, curled up, an expression of horror on her face. Jerry shook his head. She'll be no help now, he thought. Jerry opened her window, the rain beating down on him. Tossing the "would be rapists" out the window, one at a time. Catching his breath, he walked slowly towards Lulu. "Get out! She screamed at him. Jerry, please! Please! She wailed mournfully, getting up to push Jerry out the door. Jerry left, reluctantly, as he heard Lulu pushing the couch up to the door, blocking it. "Shit", Jerry said, now I'm alone again". Jerry sighed, and then went back into his room. He noticed the water level rising up almost to the stairs. It was time! He could hear the gushing water getting closer.

Jerry grabbed the backpack, pulled out the rope, and the grappling hook attached to it. He gave it a toss out the window, hoping to hook up some stable part of the roof. On the third try, the rope felt taunt. He gave it several hard yanks, and leaned into it. It held! Now how the hell am I going to get Lulu persuaded to go up it, even if it held her! Then he heard a loud crash, and water started seeping into his room. Jerry opened the door; to see the flood rushing in. he looked towards Lulus' room. The water had flooded her room, pushing her out, hanging onto the couch. Lulu screamed, hanging on to the floating couch. Several rats were clinging to her for safety. Jerry reached forward to grab her. Too late! She was pushed by the flow of water down the stairs! Lulu screamed once more, than nothing! Jerry started to cry, but pulled himself together.

The water poured in to his room., almost engulfing him. Jerry ran to the window, grasping the rope. The rush of water propelled him out the window. Jerry clung tight, being bombarded with volumes of water. Slowly, Jerry climbed up to the roof. Jerry gasping for breath reached the top. He rolled over onto the roof. Looking up, he saw the grappling hook tethered to a satellite dish. The rain poured mercilessly on him. Jerry wrapped the rope around him tightly, pulling himself up to the dish. The rain poured relentlessly for several hours. Exhausted, jerry allowed himself a nap. When he awoke, the rain had stopped! "Halleluiah", he yelled out loud. What had happened, what had changed? He thought he heard a familiar sound.

A helicopter! Jerry stood up to see. A copter was circling him! Jerry waved his hands frantically. A ladder automatically was lowered down to him. Jerry jumped on it, pulling himself up, rung by rung. As he climbed into the copter, he saw the pilot, a black woman, about his height, very trim and athletic. "No one else down there?, she asked. Jerry shook his head. Jerry observed several cages in back. They held two ducks, three dogs, and two cats. "Quite a load there", he said sitting down in the spare seat. Jerry continued, Just like Noah's Ark". The female pilot laughed. "That's funny", she said. "My father was a preacher, and he named me Noah! They both laughed. Then jerry saw…a rainbow! "What happened? He asked. "Somehow, or by Gods' hands, the moon shifted back again", she replied. "A miracle", Jerry said. They flew off together, into the rising brilliance of the sun.

Chapter IX

THE SKIN TRADERS
OF TINDALOS

The man sat alone at the table, sipping his beer. Some of the beer from the Andromeda galaxy wasn't bad, he thought. He was at a corner table, watching. "Never turn your back to the door", he said to himself. He gazed about the crowded room in tarsus, bar. Aliens and humans alike were bellied up to the bar, and sitting at some tables. Aliens from the centauries galaxy, a Snooze, who looked like a pig snout on his face, but the body, were similarly humanoid and a Zenith who was reptilian, a walked on three feet, like a tripod. Several humans, who looked like they were from Earth. Mother Earth! What a joke! Bad memories went through Bart Master's mind, shipping out on the spaceship Stairmaster. He was a twenty year man in the Marine Galaxy Space Command. A tech sergeant, in charge of weapons control had been a good gig for fifteen tears. Then on June 15, 2205, it happened! The major incident. The ship had made contact with some outlaw ships. Bart was dow in the hold, preparing the weapons.

The ship was hit broadside, knocking Bart over. He scrambled to his feet, stunned by the impact. Then he saw his best friend, Paul Deckard, coming down the stairway of the hold. "Give me a hand", Bart said to him. Paul, at five foot ten, with his military buzz cut, and steely blue eyes, smiled at him. Paul pulled his pistol out, set on stun. "Sorry, pal", he said, "Made a deal with them". Bart looked at him in surprise, as Paul pulled the trigger. Bart fell to the floor, paralyzed, but still aware. Paul came down, Pulling out some plastic explosive, and a fuse. He planted them directly onto the weapons control board. "Just think you'll get the Medal of Honor, post humously, of course". Paul smiled, "Adios, buddy, said Paul, setting the explosive

off up the stairs.

That would give him enough time to
emergency shuttle. Bart struggled with his paralyzed
mind over matter! Bart strained his muscles, his face turning
red, with exertion. At six foot five, and two seventy, he was
strong, but the stun gun held him helpless. He spied the clock
above him. 25 minutes…24 minutes.

Bart struggled on. He relaxed, thinking of his training
in meditation. The instructor had said, "Open your mind, free
it! and you will accomplish everything". Bart concentrated
his mind and will. Slowly, his body began to loosen up! Just
a little more time! He glanced at the clock. 10 more minutes!
He concentrated harder! Five minutes, three minutes! Bart
had finally unraveled his body. Jumping up, he ran for the
stairs. Too late! The explosion hit his back, driving him up
the stairs, into the main galley! Pain! Then darkness. Bart
awoke in pain. 'Oh, my god", he said. Several medics had him
tied to a hospital bed. One of them gave him an injection IV.
He started slowly drifting off. "Poor devil, he heard a female

medics' voice, He's not going to be happy, when he wakes up, or want to live".

Three Weeks Later...

Bart woke up in a daze. He had been drifting in and out of consciousness. Now he was fully awake! The pain was lesser now, but still present. Bart sat up, looking around. Then he noticed the bandages wrapped from foot to waist. What the hell! Then his hands, still heavily bandaged, travelled to his face. His head was bandaged from his face, around the back of his body, to his buttocks, and down to his legs. Damn, he thought, was there any part of him not burned! He began ripping the IVS' out, one by one. His restraining straps were loose, and he sweated, sliding his hands out. A doctor, he could tell by his white coat, and a cute blonde nurse in green scrubs, entered his room. The doctor ran over to restrain Bart. Bart pulled himself up and as the doctor got closer, he hit him squarely in the face. The doctor staggered back, trying to regain his balance. The nurse stepped forward. "Easy soldier, "she said softly, "you're safe, and you have recovered from a bad explosion". "Is everything on me burnt? ', he asked. She reached out and touched Bart's face gently. "Not everything", she said smoothly. Bart reached down to his groin. "Yes", she said, you still have the family jewels". She smiled.

The doctor had recovered from the unexpected blow. Sergeant", the doctor spoke, "I'm glad you're ok, and that hit was from your weak hand". He smiled, rubbing his nose. "What now? Bart asked. The doctor continued, "We have to put you through some strenuous physical therapy to get you at least some of your strength back". "My nose", Bart said, touching the mass of flesh. "We are going to reconstruct it", the doctor stated. He continued on, "your body was burnt very badly, but we've stopped the infection, And we'll have you in the medi-box to recover some of your tissue". Bart nodded. "When will I be able to see my body? Bart asked. "Today I'll remove your bandages", the doctor said, "but it's going to be a shock to you, so brace yourself". The nurse left, and returned with some medial tools. The doctor slowly began unwrapping him. The nurse brought in a full length mirror, then stood next to Bart. It took thirty minutes to do it. The doctor pushed the mirror closer to Bart.

Bart had closed his eyes, dreading what he would see.
he opened them. He looked like a lobster; Reddish brown
covered his face, chest and arms. He turned around,
ing over his shoulder at the back view. It was about the
, from the back of the shoulders, to his buttocks, to the
of his legs. Bart's legs started to fold up. The doctor and
the nurse grabbed him. "The dirty S.O.B.", Bart yelled out.
The nurse produced a syringe, and injected it into Bart's right
arm. He began wobbling. The doctor and nurse helped him
to bed before he collapsed. Then he passed out. Bart awoke,
to discover he was in a glass medical tank. Robotic arms were
going over his body, healing the burns. The tank was filled up
to his neck in normal saline water. The nurse came up to the
glass, and pressed her hands against it. "You doing ok, honey?
She asked. Bart could only nod. She continued, "It will take
you three weeks in there". "It's like being in your mothers'
womb". Bart wasn't sure of that, but what choice could he
have?

After three weeks, the med crew techs got Bart out.
He was shivering. The reddish brown spots were still there,
but a little more faded out. His nurse brought him a towel,

and a robe to put on. He gladly accepted it. "Now we need to fix your nose". Bart smiled at her. "What's your name? he asked. "Alana", she said smiling back. She continued, "I'm half Hawaiian, and Irish". "Nice combo", Bart said, a hula skirt, and a green leprechaun hat". Bart looked at her., thinking, She's a beautiful blonde, about five foot eight, and nice breasts. What could she see in me! Bart was in surgery for seven hours. His nose wrapped up now, would be done soon, in week, to take the bandages off. "I have a surprise for you, Alana said entering his room. She smiled. "Here ", she said, opening up a box she was carrying. A Synth suit, resembling Bart closely. "Try it on honey", she said. "How do I look? he asked her. She went out to get the full length mirror. It fit him well, even in the genital area. "The genital area of the skin is real, and functional", she grinned. "would you still like me if I didn't have this on? he asked, nervously. "I know how you feel, babe," and she said softly, approaching him. "How could you", he asked coldly.

Alana reached up behind her neck, and pulled her skin down to the waist. A Synth suit! She had horrible burn marks, on her face, and breasts! Bart stared in amazement.

She spoke quietly, "My jealous ex through acid on me. "If he couldn't have me, no one else would". She looked at Bart, empathetically. "I know how it feels", she continued, But I can't cry, the acid destroyed my tear glands". She approached Bart, and touched his groin. The skin there began to harden. He had an erection.

Alana smiled, "Mine is functional too", she whispered in his ear. They embraced, taking everything off. Then they embraced. The sex was intense, and quite good! After they climaxed, Alana got up and got dressed. "You're almost ready to leave", she said adjusting her Synth suit. It was intact, again. "You deserve a better life now", she said kissing him. Bart nodded. "here are some clothes for you", she stated, pulling out a blue tunic. "What about you", he asked, slipping into his underwear, and tunic. She smiled sadly, and said, "My place is here to help others". "It's my choice", she concluded. "Have a nice life Bart", she finalized, going out the room. Bart smiled regretfully. One of the high points in his new life just left. Bart pondered his new life, and his options.

PRESENT DAY...

Bart sat in the bar, clearing his head of past memories. The bar doors swung open. An earthman, about his height, but slimmer, came in. Behind him a Zubra, a native of planet Uropa, came in behind the earther. A Zubra, resembled a cross between a zebra, and a donkey. Brownish in color, it stood on its hind hooves as it entered. Bart was amazed that it could stand upright, at all. It was dressed in a shark skinned suit, with white tie, and blue dress shirt. This added a laughable sight. But he couldn't laugh at the Zubra. THEY were well known to be short tempered, and a strange sense of humor. Their hooves could kick you into outer space! They spied Bart in the corner, then approached him slowly. Bart slipped his laser pistol out of his jacket, and held it under the table. Friend or foe, he wasn't taking any chances. "Bart Masters, "the earthman asked, "May we speak with you? Bart nodded, keeping his hand on the trigger. The pair sat down at the table. The earthman continued, "You can put the firearm away, sergeant, we mean you no harm".

Bart looked wary. The earthman continued, tapping his eyes, "Infra red vision implants". He continued, "I am the assistant director of G.S.S., Galactic Secret Service". "My friend here is Major Zen, of our military branch". The Zubra he hawed at Bart. Bart tensed up. "Sorry, force of habit", the Zubra apologized. Bart relaxed, setting the laser pistol on the table. "What does G.S.S., want with me? Bart asked. "My name is Jed Barstow, and we want you to go on a mission". Bart laughed. "I'm on disability, not a soldier anymore". "We know all that", the Zubra brayed, dismissal in his voice. 'Not interested", Bart retorted. "We want to make you an offer", Jed stated. Bart decided to sit and listen. Jed continued, "There is a black market in synth suits.

They are cheap, and wear out in three months". He continued on, they've gone to soldiers, witness protection, and survivors of accidents, unfortunately". This had Barts' attention now. Jed said, "The synth suits come from outlaws, on the planet Tindalos". Bart asked, who? Jed looked grim, and replied, "Your old pal Deckard. "He runs the whole show". Bart was startled. Jed said, "I knew you'd be interested." "Damn right!" Bart said, grinding his teeth. "What else? Bart asked. Jed replied, "They have Chang So". "They've kidnapped him". He continued, they're making him create the cheap suits". "But now for Deckard's' men, they make them better". He concluded, "That way they can infiltrate anywhere they go". Chang So! The creator of the synth suit. No wonder they stole him away. "So are you in? the Zubra brayed. "Yes", Bart replied. "I want two million space credits and one of those Synth suits". The pair at the table exchanged looks. "Done", Jed said, "When can you start? Bart stood up. "Tomorrow, if I can get a partner to help, and some special equipment. "Ok, ", brayed the major, "That's my end". A pair of earthers, judging by their appearance walked in. One was very tall, and dark. The other was white and shorter, with a buzzed haircut. They wore sleek, mid length leather jackets.

Bart's sense of menace became alert. The two earthers withdrew automatic laser rifles from their jackets. "Hit the deck! Bart roared, as he tipped over the table. The first volley of shits, hit the wall behind the trio. Bart opened fire, springing into action. Another volley of shots from the earthers sprang out. Jed was hit in the arm, almost severing it. Bart fired at the tall dark one, its impact blowing a hole through his skull! The shorter one was starting to reload. The Zubra pranced forward, like a show horse. Lifting its front hooves, he kicked the man in the head, making a loud thump! The man, his head crushed, fell to the ground; his body shaking in reflex from the impact, then stopped moving. 'Wow! Bart said admiringly.

He spoke on, "help me with Jed, his arm was badly hurt, but the laser had cauterized it some." Bart and the major helped Jed to his feet. The crowd in the bar was hiding under tables and chairs. One of the Snozes stood up, having pissed his pants, and very red faced. "I'll get Jed to the medic. "We'll catch up with you later. ", the Zubra said. "Very impressive", Bart said. He asked, "What do your men call you? The Zubra replied, "Major Asshole, he grinned, but not to my face". He grinned. The Zubra brayed, and then helped Jed out the door. He helped Jed up onto his back, and began trotting down the road. The sound of clipity clops of his feet echoed. Bart left shortly after. He returned to his room, and waited. It was several days later before he was contacted. His job as a cargo handler on outbound ships was easy. He had finished earlier in the day. There was a clip clop up his stairs, then a knock. It had to be the major! Bart picked up his pistol, just to be sure.

He opened the door cautiously. "Hello, Sergeant", the Zubra said. "May I come in? Bart put his pistol in his pocket, and motioned to the Zubra to come in. "How's Jed", Bart asked him. The major his girth too big to sit in a chair, popped his tail end on the floor, with a woof! The major grunted. "He's better, being fitted for a bionic arm". Bart nodded. The Major continued, "We found a leak in the network, and took care of the spy". He grimaced, "I took care of him myself".

Bart tried to not imagine the spy's' demise. 'I'm having equipment shipped to your room", the Major said. He drew out a long list out of his suit pocket. "See if you need need anything else. Bart glanced at the list…

1. High powered infra red binoculars

2. MPG high powered rifle.

3. Neuro net connectors, with neuro net screen.

4. New improved synth suit, for a disguise.

5. Plastic explosives.

6.   Self injector for Neuro net connection

7.   Invisible body armor.

"Looks like everything", Bart said. "I'd like to get a hold of an old friend". "Who? The Major asked. "Marta Rey", Bart responded. "The Merc", the major said. "Yes", came Bart's answer, she is an independent contractor, now". "Are you sure", the major brayed, She's very…unpredictable." "Not with me, she isn't", Bart grinned. The major nodded, then left. Several days later, there was a knock at the door. The postal person was a female! She looked familiar! "Here's your order", she said, carrying several large boxes in. Now he recognized her! It was Marta! "Hi sweet thing", Bart said to her, "How's business? "Can't disguise my voice", she replied, stepping into Bart's room with the packages. She took off her postal uniform revealing a skin tight leather outfit which covered her from breasts, to her thighs. At five eight, and about one twenty, she was still in great shape, her long dark hair covered her breasts, nicely. He noticed she had some new devices, and upgrades installed. She had polished combat boots on her feet. She stood there, as Bart continued admiring her. She found a chair to sit in. "You're the only S.O.B. that can call me that, without missing his balls". She smiled sweetly at him. "I can believe that", Bart said, grinning back at her.

He continued, "I haven't seen you since the Mars problem". She replied, stretching her long legs "that was fun; this is going to be damn hard work". Bart looked her over. She had a cybernetic eye installed on the right one. It could monitor and record videos, without interfering with her vision. On her long fingernails were injectable needles, either set for paralysis or kill. Her MP5 was strapped to her side. "Same old shit", she declared, with a few refined touches". Bart smiled again. "Let's see what goodies you brought me". Bart and Marta started opening the packages. It was all there! Plus a few extras. Several frag grenades, and a retractable bowie knife. As the pair examined their prizes, someone knocked on the door. Clop! Clop! It was the Major! "Come in, doors open", Bart said. The major entered, looking at the two. "You look like something I could ride", she commented. The Major brayed, "how about the other way around", he grinned. "Not if you want to end up a gelding", she retorted. The major brayed again, Guess not! He turned to Bart. "Is it everything you asked for? Bart replied "It's good". The major nodded. There was a rush of footsteps coming up the stairs. "Incoming!' the Major yelled, drawing his laser pistol. Bart and Marta produced their firearms. Something hit the floor by the apartment door. "Duck or bleed', yelled the Major as he spread out on the floor. The explosion rocked the apartment.

The door has been destroyed, leaving a gaping hole where it used to be. The major and the duo stood up. They began firing towards the hole where the door once stood. Four men came rushing in. Typical outlaw wear, dressed in all metallic black. They began firing. The major fired a blast, dropping the first one. Bart and Marta returned fire to the other three. They hit two, dismembering them. The last one ran down the stairs. "Shit! "He'll probably go for backup", the major said loudly. "Lets get out of here!" Bart exclaimed. His ears still ringing from the explosion. Bart and Marta began gathering up the equipment. "Guess you'll need that ride now", the Major brayed. He got down on all fours. Bart and Marta glanced at each other. Then they slowly climbed up the back of the Zubra. "Are you sure? Marta asked. 'I can get you out of here faster", the major snorted. "And away we GO! Shouted the major. "Hold on tight". The Zubra began galloping out the hole, and down the stairs. They hit the street, moving quickly. Bart glanced around, seeing the man who had escaped. He had gone and gathered up two more companions. They started firing at the two on the majors back.

Bart swung around backwards on the Zubra, and began returning fire. Bart hit one, shattering him. His aim wasn't great, harder to hit a moving target. The major was hit by a glancing shot in his left flank. He stumbled than fell. "Sorry", he said, laying there. "find Jed, he'll help you". The Major said, sprawled out on the street. "I'll hold them off, till you get clear. "What about you", she asked. "I'll be ok", he said, then continued, "I expect a strip show later". Marta smiled, "You Got It! Bart and Marta took off down the street, running. The last they saw saw of the Major, he was half sitting up, firing his pistol at the two enemies gaining on them. Bart and Marta ran for at least they came to a vid station, where they could make a call. Gasping for breath, Bart hit the keyboard, on display there. "Operator", a voice said, "text, or hologram? Bart replied, "Hologram", and then punched in a secret code, the Major had told him. Then Bart punched in [privacy}.

The screen became clearer, and the hologram appeared. "What happened? Jed asked, displaying his newly planted bionic arm. "Great work, huh? he asked, holding his bionic arm up to view. "Yes, "Bart said, then explained the situation to him. "Damn", Jed said angrily, "I'll send a team to help the major ASAP". He continued, it's on its way, Five minutes tops". He went on "Go to 1233 Echo Drive, it's a safe house, in the country". Jed gave them directions. "Take a private shuttle', Jed said, "Give them this number". "Tell the robo cab, 7653x, that will get you there". Jed looked at the pair, "Time to go, someone is trying to hack me! The screen went dead. The pair hailed a cab going by. "How can I help you? it asked, in its mechanized grating voice. Bart gave it the code. "Yes sir! it replied, "Top security! It opened the doors to the cab, and the two got in. The cab raced off at high speed, dodging traffic. Ten minutes later, they had arrived at their destination. A huge grey mansion, with steel gates surrounding it, and lots of Evergreen bushes surrounded the mansion almost obscuring it. The steel gates creaked open, admitting them. The cab pulled up to the mansion. Its white pillars glowing in the daytime. Bart and Marta exited the cab, slowly walking towards the mansion. Jed appeared, Dressed in the Blue and yellow uniform, with G.S.S. labeled across it. He held a device in his hand, a device in his hand, a small rectangular black box. He pushed a series of buttons on it. The glowing pillars dimmed. "Come on in", Jed said, waving his bionic arm. "I've lowered the defense shield". He continued, "If someone had tried to enter, a laser beam would have dispatched them". Bart and Marta agreed, nodding their heads.

They stepped up to Jed, on the mahogany porch. "How are you? Bart asked pointing at the bionic arm. "It's good", Jed replied, except when I need to piss, I have to be careful. Jed smiled, and Bart and Marta grinned. "This way", Jed motioned to them. As they entered, they gazed at the huge front room. At least 100 feet long and 30 feet high. They noticed the beautiful paintings on the wall. Bart guessed, originals, not copies. "Come into the library", Jed motioned to a door on the right. They entered the large maple wood door. There were several leather couches and chairs. A bookcase case eight feet high, with many volumes clad in leather bound, and even paperbound! Marta went over to survey the books, as Bart parked himself into a soft leather chair.

Jed sat in a chair opposite of him. "Let's begin", Jed said. Bart nodded, and Marta returned from the bookcase, to sit in a chair next to Bart. Jed cleared his throat. "Backup arrived in time to help the major", he said. "Good! Bart and Marta said, in unison. "Yes", Jed went on, "When backup arrived in time for the major, one enemy was dead, shot in the stomach, and the other had his legs crushed by the major's hind legs". Bart and Marta grinned. Jed continued, "The Major is in rehab now, but should get better in a few days." "What now? Marta asked. Jed cleared his throat again. "We had the prisoner brought here for interrogation". "Would you like to help? Jed asked the two. Bart and Marta nodded in agreement, Jed went to the bookcase, and slid one of the books forward.

The bookcase moved, revealing a passageway, and a stairs. "Follow me", Jed said entering. They went down a long flight of spiraling stairs. Hall lights had appeared as soon as they entered. They reached the bottom, and looked around. A cement floor, with only a metal chair, and a table. On the table sat a neuro net device. The hookups for it lay nearby. In the chair, sat one of the men who had attacked them. His legs looked horribly crushed. Through his pain, gritting his teeth, he looked at the trio. "who are you? He asked, grunting. "Are you the bad guy? he asked Bart. "Wrong! Marta stated, coming towards him. "I'm the bad ass", she concluded. She stepped on the man's crushed legs. "You bitch! He hollered, tears in his eyes. "Oh! Marta replied, "I'm much worse than that! Jed spoke up, "Enough! I got a better way to get him to talk". "Be sure he's strapped down good". "What the hell for! the man yelled, 'I'm not going anywhere! "You'll see", Jed replied. "Have you installed your neuro net connection yet? Jed asked Bart. How about you< Marta? "Absolutely", Marta replied. Jed plugged into the black box, running three wires from it. One to the box, one connected to Marta, and one to the prisoner. "So he has a connection? Bart remarked. "Now he does", Jed replied. Jed adjusted the cable to the back of the man's head. "Hell no! the man exclaimed, trying to twist around. The straps held the man tightly. Marta and the man were jacked in. "I'll make a copy of his brain waves, and send them to you", Jed explained. The machine came to alert, flashing its many colored lights.

The man stiffened his body, and then relaxed. Marta grinned as the waves came through on feedback. copying the man's memories. "Ew" You've been a naughty boy, she said, 'having sex with a Venusian Tri sexual". She laughed. "What's that? Bart asked. "Ok, I got it all", she said. She continued, "You can store it now". She turned to Bart 'There's a visual here you don't want to see about the trisexual". Jed said, "Remove your cable, Marta". Marta did so. Then Jed pushed some red buttons on the box. The man's body began jerking, convulsing, then stopped. "What did you do to him? Bart asked. Jed had removed the cable from the box and the man. "Erasure of memories", Jed replied. He went on, "He's now just an amnesiac, suffering from P.T.S.D.". "Damn! Marta exclaimed, "What will you do with him now? Jed replied, "Ship him off to a mental facility in the Ceres section, for the rest of his life." Marta shuddered. "Hey! Jed said, "It's better than being eliminated". Bart spoke up" Almost the same as". They returned up the stairs, where Jed made a call on his vid phone. "Prisoner transfer, he spoke into the phone. He continued, "Location 212". Jed heard an affirmative on the phone, and then hung up. "Let's see what we got from his memories", Jed stated, placing the box on a table in front of him. He brought out a blue box, and a remote device. He hooked up the back box to the blue one. Then he aimed the remote at the opposite wall from them. The wall folded in, revealing a full video screen. Jed pushed another button on the remote. The screen came to life! The images flickered, blurring on the screen. "Need to adjust it", Jed said, pushing another button. The images and the images began to sharpen up. Let's skip the Venusian tri sexual part", Bart suggested. Marta laughed, "Aren't you curious? "Not that!, Bart exclaimed. Jed laughed too. "Ok, Jed said, "I'll fast forward it past that". Jed skipped through some scenes. Then he came across a starship nestled in an industrial factory. "That's got to be it", Bart commented. Marta said "Look at the skyline". Three moons! Damn, Marta thought that was Tindalos! Bart said "Yep". An outlaw planet!"

The only rules were there is none! Bart continued, "He who has the most cash, and force, rule there! Marta nodded. "We'll have to go in incognito, at least me", Bart said. "Try on your synth suit, Bart", Jed insisted. "I'm not shy", Marta smiled. Bart stripped off his old suit, and began putting on the new one. "That son of a bitch Deckard needs to die painfully", Marta remarked, looking at Bart's burnt body. Bart continued pulling on the new suit, ignoring Marta's remark. Then he dressed in his blue coveralls. "Here, look Jed said, leading Bart over to a mirror in the corner of the room. Bart gazed into the mirror. "Wow! Bart thought, Amazing! Now he had dark skin, and had long hair braided like an Rasfarian. "I think I like that", Marta said. "Cool", Jed remarked, thumbs up in a high sign. Jed continued, "Your name is Jaffa Allred, a Jamaican expatriate from earth, living in the Ceres section." He continued, "You are a Master Card Handler, "I have your Masters' card, Id, and passport". "What am I? Marta asked. Jed smiled, "You are his shipping associate". He continued, "I have your id, and papers here". Jed handed them the faked documents, and papers. They returned to the vid screen. Three doors to the facility. Front, side, and left, and a cargo door. "Simple enough", Bart said, "I can work with this". Then Bart spied Deckard entering the facility. His hands clenched tightly, and his face turned a cherry red. "Easy now", Marta said soothingly, He'll get his soon!" She continued, "Don't make it to personal, or it will screw up the mission. Bart relaxed, concentrating on the screen. "I know where to plant the explosives", Bart stated. "One in the ships nuclear chamber, one in the factories' first floor, and one up Deckard's ass, if I find him". Jed smiled, and began, "you'll need to practice your accent". He continued, I have vids for you to watch, on shipping procedures, and so forth", he said to Marta.

The work had just begun. Bart found the accent training helpful, and he was a natural! Marta went through over a thousand boring files on shipping procedures. Jed walked in while Marta was finishing the files. She looked up from her desk. "What about Chang?" So, she asked. Jed replied, "We think he's sequestered in the computer room of the spaceship". He continued, "Be Bart doesn't get carried away, and blow it up before we can get Chang". Marta replied, "I don't think he'd jeopardize the mission, but I'll keep a close watch on him". Jed nodded his head, then left.

Bart and Marta were ready to leave. Their small three man cruiser was getting ready to leave. Tindalos was only twelve light years away. They could jump into hyperspace, and get there in 36 hours. Bart and Marta were ready to go. They entered the ship. It was bright cobalt, metallic object, with Jamaican lettering on it. Its' name was "Yeh, Maan, on the side. As they stepped into the ship, they saw their pilot! A Venusian tri sexual! "Oh, Great", Bart remarked. The Venusian was dressed in baggy yellow pants, probably to conceal its questionable private parts. The Venusians tunic was a loose, metallic tunic, where its four arms, two on each side, protruded. 'Greetings, humanoids, It chattered, with an eerie combination of male/female voice. "Hi, Honey!", Marta smiled. Bart nodded. Better not piss off the pilot, he thought. It could drop them off straight into a volcanic planet, or something worse! "I am Zervax, your pilot', it quipped. Bart and Marta sat down in the passenger seats behind the Venusian.

Bart and Marta had heard that the Venusians had great ability as pilots. Its four arms. In ambidextrous ability, could Multi task, especially during flight emergencies. They were probably safer than a human pilot could be. "Shall we ascend? Zervax asked. Zervax continued, "Strap yourself in, which means you handsome", the Venusian instructed Bart. Bart kept his mouth shut, and Marta had already buckled in. The ceiling at G.S.S. building opened up, as the ship began to rise. It ascended slowly, at first until it reached the opening.

In a quick flash, the Venusian flew them through the air, into space, leaving only a small dot of the planet they had just left. Bart and Marta were speechless! "Damn, it's good! Bart remarked to Marta. Marta smiled nervously. "I have a p1 rating", the Venusian said, turning to the two. P1 was the highest honor bestowed on a pilot. Bart and Marta were impressed. Zervax set the ship to autopilot. Then Zervax unstrapped himself from the pilots' chair. "How safe is that?, Marta asked, pointing to the pilot. "We are moving in a northwestern direction "Zervax commented. The Venusian continued, "Autopilot on, meteor detector on, and collision avoidance on". It smiled. "You haven't worked with a Venusian before? The two nodded. The Venusian went on, "We will work well together, I think".

Bart and Marta nodded in the affirmative. "I'm easy to get along with". "Always professional, but only when I'm on duty "Zervax smiled. "Still after everything gets completed, I have needs to be taken care of, it smiled crookedly. "Sorry, not my thing", Marta said. "Same here, nothing personal", Bart added. "Ok, the venusian said, "Food and drink in the galley". The Venusian pointed towards the aft part of the ship.

The three sat around the table, enjoying a meal, and drinking some earth brandy. All three avoided any talking about sex, and began studying their mission. Zervax produced a map of Tindalos. "I'll land you there", Zervax said, pointing to an area two miles south of their target. Zervax continued, "You'll have to hump it from there". Bart asked, "Will they see us when we land? "No, Zervax replied, "I have a sonar device that will bounce off any signals, or EMPS". Bart and Marta agreed. "What about you? Marta asked. "I'll be stationed above the atmosphere, in hiding", Zervax replied. "Just signal with this, when plan is executed". The Venusian handed Bart a small red circular button that he could pin to his tunic. "Press that, and I'll be on my way to back you up". Bart and Marta nodded in unison. "We should be there tomorrow", Zervax said. It continued, "Try to get some rest". There was fold out bunks attached to the bulkhead. "What about you? Bart asked. "I'll just nod in the pilots' chair, just to be sure everything ok". Zervax continued, "I only need three hours sleep. "It's a biological thing".

Bart and Marta turned their bunks down. They tried to get some rest. Marta tossed and turned in her sleep. Bart had dreamed about finally meeting up with Deckard. He awoke several times, and fell back to sleep. Just about to start dreaming again, He heard an alarm. "Outlaw ship at twelve o clock", the Venusian hollered. Bart and Marta struggled up out of their bunks, and came forward. They looked at the sonar screen. "We're being hailed", the Venusan said. A voice came over the intercom. "Ship, identify yourself", a gravelly voice spoke. "Looks like a scout ship, left here for defense", Marta said. The Venusian pressed the intercom button. "I'm a Venusan, bringing sex toys to Tindalos", Zervax replied. "Stay there", growled the voice, "I'm going to scan you". "Shit! The Venusian said, "They'll know we have weapons aboard! Zervax set the H missiles on readiness. "Who the hell are you? Boomed the voice from the speaker.

The Venusian replied calmly, "A Venusian who says you can kiss the back cheeks of both my butts, in unison! Bart looked at Zervax. Butts? Damn, he didn't need to know that! Zervax fired three missiles at the ship, dead on. Then the Venusian raised his force field. The force field wasn't necessary, as Zervax caught them by surprise. The outlaw scout exploded into a thousand pieces. Some debris had hit the force field, but didn't penetrate it. "To close", Marta said. "Yes", Zervax responded, we'd better hurry up to Tindalos". Zervax concluded, "It will take a while before they are reported missing". "Shit happens, in space", Bart said, grinning. They continued on their journey, finally reaching Tindalos. Zervax implemented the security software, and slowly descended to the planet below. Hovering at five feet above ground, Bart and Marta bailed out. They landed on some soft green grass, apparently in an abandoned field. Poppies! Bart saw. Ripe for the picking to produce Heroin! Another business of Deckard's, he thought. The two began hiking down a path, with thirty pound backpacks strapped to them.

They continued towards the factory, moving swiftly. They hadn't encountered anyone yet. Pausing on the edge of the field, the duo paused for a rest. "Hyper space made me a little wobbly", Bart said, sitting down on the grass. "Yep!", Marta said, "It happened in our sleep". She continued, it messed me up a little too". They sat there for a few minutes. "We have to hide our gear", Marta stated. Bart looked around for a suitable spot. He spotted a large Oleander bush, on the right. "There", he pointed, "That Oleander is poisonous". He took off his backpack. "No one will bother it", he continued "Not even the animals". Marta agreed. They both slid their backpacks under the bush, avoiding not touching the sides. "Ready to head in", Bart asked. "Anytime", replied Marta.

They continued on to the factory, only carrying their laser pistols on their side. When they reached the factory, several guards stood around it. Bart announced them. "I'm' Jaffa allredd, and this is my assistant Janna". "We are cargo specialists". "Wait a minute", one of the guards said, stepping into the factory. He returned with a giant of a man! Taller than Bart, very muscular, with a shaved head, black goatee, and a laser rifle slung over his shoulder. He was dressed in all black, one piece blue tunic, and combat style boots. "What do you want?, he hollered, asking them. "We are cargo specialists, looking for work." "Fuck off,", the man said, "We already have two".

A man appeared behind him. "Let them in, the man behind him said, "Let's see what they can do". It was Deckard! Bart recognized him immediately. Short dark hair, military style, steel eyes, about Bart's height, but slimmer, by about twenty kilos. Bart suppressed his anger, unclenching his hands. The duo walked forward into the factory. A huge complex, about two hundred feet long, one hundred feet high, with a retractable roof, large enough to exit a starship. Production work was going on, stamping out synth suits by the hundreds. Behind that was a large, glass enclosed lab, problem for producing Heroin. Men in there were wearing respirators, scurrying back and forward among the tubes and vials sitting along a steel table.

Bart and Marta took in the scene. Incredible! Large mounted production! I wonder where they kept Chang So, Marta thought. Bart smiled, "I'll get you", he whispered softly. Deckard spoke "So what can you do for me?, he asked. Marta replied, "Show me your books, and I can tell you". "We beat dem bad'. {Surpass}, said Bart speaking rasfarian. "Jamaican, huh?, Deckard asked, "Can you speak universal English, he asked. "A mi feel tell you", Bart replied, "Yes, I can ", Bart concluded., in English. Deckard escorted them to his office, on the right of them. "Show me", Deckard said, pointing to a row of computer terminals lined up on a long oak table there. "All right, Marta said, jumping onto the computers, keyboarding.

In a few minutes, she found what she was looking for. "Your cargo man, and shipper are skimming off the bottom from you!, she stated flatly. "How's that!, questioned Deckard, his eyes burning with anger. "He's shipping out on the cheap, and pocketing the difference", Marta replied, smiling. "Both the cargo man and the shipper are in collusion with this". Deckard left the room, stomping his feet.

He returned with two guards, holding the cargo man and the shipper held tightly by the guards. "A sod I ting set {that's right}, in Jamaican. "Explain this! Dekard demanded, pointing at the computer terminals. "What the hell! The cargo man said, "I didn't do this". "Bullshit! Deckard exclaimed, "The evidence proves it". But...but... the shipper stuttered. "Nobody cheats me", Deckard stated. "Take them out and shoot them, then burn their bodies". He continued, "Show it to rest of the men to let them know, I mean business! The guards dragged them out screaming and yelling! Then Bart and Marta heard several blasts from laser pistols. "A so di ting set", breathed Bart out. "Ok", Deckard said to the two, "You're hired". "500 credits a week then if you do anything better I'll increase it 10%". Deckard continued, "I think you're smart enough not to screw with me! Bart and Marta nodded in agreement. "Now how about you", He turned to Bart. "Let's see your cargo setup". Bart said, using a hint of his accent.

Deckard escorted Bart to the cargo hold. It was still kind of archaic, but functional, and slow. "You need an anti-grav device to move things faster"< Bart commented. "Hard to get now a days, without a lot of red tape"< Deckard said. "I can do", Bart said confidently. Bart continued, "Give me a few days". Deckard nodded and said, "Upstairs are a private room on the left. "You and your other can bunk there". Marta had finished the accounts, and joined Bart upstairs in the private room. There was a series of fluorescent lights, burning. Also a queen sized bed, plus a computer setup. Marta checked for listening devices. She found three! One under the computer desk, one hooked into the computer, and one under the bed! "What a perv", Marta commented. Bart grinned. "Intimate talk about business, sometimes happens in bed". Marta grinned, and then began disabling the listening devices. "Just for a short time", Marta said, or otherwise they'll know what's up". Bart responded, "Maybe they'll think it's a short, as long as it lasts only a few minutes".

Using a portable jammer hidden in her clothes, she promptly jammed the three signals. "Quick", Bart said to her. Marta replied, we have seen their illegal activities". "But, she continued, I have to find out where they are keeping Chang So". Bart agreed. Tomorrow they would start in earnest. For now, Marta released the jammer, and Bart and she went to bed. It was 2200 now, a good time to rest, to get up early at o600. Bart and Marta sexed briefly, and then fell asleep into each others' arms. Day was barely creeping up when they awoke. "I have a way to contact someone about the ant-grav device device", Bart explained to Marta. "Good", Marta replied, slipping on her clothes, as Bart got dressed. "Today begins", he stated, heading out the door. "Me too", Marta said, going out behind him. Marta continued, "I have to check the accounts, she grinned. They both were busy that day. Marta was secretly going to transfer Deckard's' accounts to G.S.S. Bart went to the loading docks to check things out.

A man sat in a chair dozing in front of the monitor, while cargo was being jammed up. It was the bald man he had met before. "What the hell do you want", the bald man said, waking up, rubbing his eyes. "No sleeping on the job",

Bart said, pointing at the jam on the conveyor. "Who the fuck are you", the man growled, standing up. He was a big man, outweighing Bart by twenty kilos. Deckard appeared behind Bart. "What's going on", he demanded. "This fish {homosexual} is sleeping on the job, causing a jam up on the conveyor, Bart replied. "What did you call me? the bald man asked, demandingly. "He says you're a cocksucker", Deckard grinned. The bald mans' face turned red. He advanced quickly on Bart. "Why you...", he began clenching his fists. Bart gave him a swift kick to the groin. The man gasped, falling to his knees. Bart then clipped him once in the face, knocking out the mans' front row of teeth. Then he collapsed. "Damn! Deckard exclaimed, "I only know a man once who fought that similar style ". Deckard looked at Bart curiously. "Where is he now", Bart asked. "Unfortunately, dead", Deckard replied, smiling, "A good friend". Bart thought, A good friend my ass! "Well then it's not me, man, Bart returned. "No, he was Anglo, strange though", Deckard commented.

He eyed Bart strangely, then said, "You take his job, and be supervisor too". He continued, "I'll double your pay". Deckard strode off. The two guards came in, and hauled the bald man away. Bart continued monitoring the shipping all day. I think he's getting suspicious of me, Bart thought. Marta and I will have to take action soon. At the end of the day, Bart met up with Marta. "I think he's become suspicious of us", he said. "Why? she asked. "He thinks I act a lot like Bart", he replied. "we'll have to go ahead soon", Marta whispered. Deckard appeared. "Why don't the two of you go take a shuttle into town"? He continued, "You could use a break". The two glanced at each other. Marta said, "Sounds like fun". The town shuttle arrived in front of the factory.' that evening. It was getting darker. The shuttle doors opened up. "Welcome to Tindalos Shuttle INC. ', Boomed a robotic voice, coming from its' stereophonic speakers.

The duo stepped in, found their seats, and strapped in. "get ready for a bumpy ride", the voice said, like an old movie star of the twentieth century. The shuttle zoomed off, at breakneck speed. Cruising along at 200 kilometers a minute, they reached the town in no time. "Your arrival", boomed the voice, and then added, "have a good time! Tindalos town was named Pirate Haven. It was a small area of rundown buildings. The two spotted a sign, flashing its neon, saying,

OUTLAW NEST BAR. "sounds good', Bart said to Marta. Marta quipped, "Do you think Deckard is searching our room? "Absolutely", Bart replied, "But he'll find nothing out of the ordinary". Marta nodded. They entered the bar. Assorted aliens sat around the chairs in the bar, and the counters.

They were drinking and talking loud to each other. Bart observed several Snozes, some Zinths, and a few Earthers. The two found a table in the far north corner, and sat down. A barmaid, dressed in a long billowy robe, with straight dark hair past her shoulders, approached them. "Hi, sweeties", she said, in a familiar tone to the two. They both looked startled. It was the Venusian. "Need a drink. "I'm here to serve you", the Venusian said, winking. Bart spoke to the Venusian quietly. "What are you doing here?, he asked. The Venusian grinned sheepishly. "A girl/guy has to have some fun". The Venusian looked solemnly, "When? Zervax asked. "Tonight", replied Bart "Are you ready? "Damn straight", Zervax replied. "About 2200", Bart stated. Bart continued, "I think Deckard is on to us". Zervax nodded, "I'll get you some Tindalos ale", He/ she said.

The bartender, a Quirk, with a huge face of a duck, and humanoid arms, glared at Zervax. "The boss is calling," Zervax said. The Venusian returned with the ale, pale, frothy, and ice cold. "Is your boss mad at you? Marta asked. "Nah!, returned Zervax, "I'll give him something special in a while, and he'll get over it". Marta grinned, and Bart smirked. They finished their ale, and had two more. It was 2030 by then. "We'd better go", Marta suggested. A Zenith got into an argument with the bartender. The Zenith spit into the bartenders' face. The bartender jumped over the counter, and started swinging on the Zenth. "Nothing like a good fight", Bart said. He continued, "Let's get out of here! They left, catching the shuttle at 2045, heading back. Bart gave the shuttle different coordinates. The shuttle hesitated. "Fix it!, Bart told Marta. Marta reached over the control panel. Removing it, she crossed some wires. "Damage to property is punishable as a felony", boomed the robotic voice, then it quieted.

The shuttle arrived at the edge of the woods. Bart and Marta exited. "I will notify the authorities", the robotic voice stated. "Bullshit", Bart replied, destroying the control panel.

Rendering the shuttle useless."That's the end of that", Bart grinned. The two retrieved their backpacks, and headed for the factory. Reaching their destination, they drew their laser pistols. Some people were loading cargo onto the ship. Bart turned to Marta. "Go look for Chang So, ', he said, "And here is some explosive charges, ". Marta took them, and tucked them into a hidden pocket of her tunic. Bart crept slowly around to the Heroin lab. Good! Only one guy in a white lab coat was present. Bart knocked on the glass window. The lab man looked up irritated. "The boss wants to see you now!, demanded Bart. As the lab man stepped out, Bart grabbed, putting pressure on him. The man gasped, and collapsed to the ground. Bart entered the lab. A large container of Heroin, sat in front of him. He quickly planted the explosives, and set the timer. One Hour! It better be enough time! Bart left, heading towards the entrance on the left. Then they planted more explosives there., and set the timer.

Meanwhile, Marta headed in towards the ships' entrance. The bald man, who had no front teeth, glared at her. "what do you want!, he demanded. "How about a tour, then I'll give you something good", she said, seductively. "Like what? He asked but looked curious. She gently grasped his groin. 'How about some of this, in me", she grinned. "Ok', he responded, putting his arm around her. They entered the ship. Only one man using the ships' controls. Marta smiled seductively at the bald man. She opened her tunic exposing her pert breasts. The bald man stared greedily at them. He began massaging her breasts. "Hmm, yes!, she whispered in his ear. Slowly, she reached for the combat knife hidden in her robe. Quickly she stabbed him repeatedly in his stomach, and groin. He cried out once, then hit the floor with a dull thud! The man at the control panel jumped up, reaching for his laser pistol. Marta moved cat like towards him, slashing his throat open. The man began gurgling, swallowing blood, then collapsed to the floor. Marta moved quickly trough the ship. Searching several compartments, she found Chang in a large computer room. His back was turned away from her. He heard her footsteps behind him. Chang, Chinese national, stood only about five foot six, slender, wearing gold rim glasses. The glasses hung crooked on his head. "I'm almost done now", he said. "Come with me if you want to get away", she said. Chang startled, turned around to face her. "what the hell!, he exclaimed, seeing her covered in blood. "Some of your friends didn't want you to leave. "The bloods theirs, not mine! She continued, "I'm from the G.S.S., hear to rescue you." "Hell yes", Chang said getting up rapidly on his feet. "'Follow me, and stay behind me", she instructed him. Chang So countered, "Give me a weapon, and I'll help! She looked at him. "Hey!, he said to her, I was a space ranger in the Andromeda wars, when I was younger". Marta smiled at him admiringly. "I'll get you one from one of the dead outlaws". Chang followed her. "Do you know how to plant these?, she asked him., removing the explosives from her tunic. Chang grabbed them, then wired them into the control panel of the ship.

He set the timer for thirty minutes. Chang reached down and retrieved a laser pistol from the dead control room man. "Let's go", he stated. Arming himself the pistol. They continued to the cargo bay. Bart on the other hand, was slowly advancing towards Deckard's' office. He crept up to the door, and slowly opened it. Deckard stood there, laser pistol in his hand. "Who are you?, he asked demandingly, his finger tight on the trigger. Bart removed the top half of his Synth suit, revealing his damaged body. "When you want to kill a man, be sure he's dead! Bart continued, "Look at me in the eye, Paul! Deckard gasped in surprise, realizing who Bart was! "You're just a freak show... now!, Deckard stuttered, still in shock from seeing Bart. Bart saw the advantage! He quickly grasped his laser pistol. Both men fired at the same time. Both were off at their aim. Bart took one in his left arm, but laser from Bart had shattered Deckard's shoulder. Yelling in pain, Deckard bailed through the glass window of his office.

Only two floors up, he hit the ground running! Bart in some pain, but still active, ran down the stairs after him. He observed Marta and Chang confronting a dozen men at the cargo hold. "Marta said, "Let's do it, you S.O. Bs". Chang repeated the same. There was a barrage of laser fire. Marta got a glancing shot to her right leg. Chang was still intact. Then, they all heard the roar of a jet pack suit. It was Zervax, holding pistols in all four hands. "Yippee!, he yelled, firing on the outlaws., killing at least two. Deckard and Bart exchanged fire. Then Deckard spied Zervax. He fired a blast, hitting the jet pack, blowing it up. The Venusian screamed, then plummeted to the floor. "Damn you", Bart swore. Marta and Chang had cleaned up the other outlaws. That just left

Deckard! Deckard made a break for it, running towards his private shuttle stationed outside. He bailed into the doors, it not completed shutting.

Bart jumped up, clinging to the doors. Deckard tried prying Bart's fingers off the doors. Hanging on Bart laid a swift kick to Deckard's groin. Deckard fell back onto the floor of the shuttle. Bart pulled himself in, aiming his laser pistol at Deckard. Deckard jumped up, laser pistol in his hand. They both fired simultaneously. Nothing! The laser pistols were out of commission. Bart threw his pistol down. Deckard did also. "I wonder what we'll do now", asked Deckard, retrieving a combat knife from his boot. Bart did the same. They approached each other circling, eye to eye contact. Deckard made a slashing motion at Bart, aiming for his throat. Bart paired, slicing at Deckard's arm, opening it up. Men grunted, slicing pairing, and thrusting. A cut here, a cut there! Deckard slipped, cursing. Bart stepped in slicing a section of Deckard's stomach open. Deckard hit the floor, holding his gut in. "I guess this it", Deckard wheezed. "Not quite", Bart said, staring down at him. Deckard looked questionably at him. Bart messed with the wires to the nuclear generator that powered the ship. An alarmed robotic voice bellowed out. "D anger, danger! Overload! Overload! Deckard gave Bart a hostile stare. The shuttle began slowing to a reasonable pace. Bart looked at Deckard, "see around pal", he said, bailing out the shuttles doors. "Yeh, in hell!, Deckard announced.

Bart hit the ground running. H e got up and took at least a mile away. He turned toward the shuttle,. The shuttle exploded into a fiery bonfire, producing a mushroom cloud in the air. Bart gasping for breath, satisfied, started hiking back to the factory. There he met Marta and Chang, waiting. "Let's get out of here", Marta suggested. They moved away from the factory about two miles. Marta produced a remote detonating device. "Here goes", she said, pushing the button. Silence, then an ear splitting roar, and a cloud of smoke rose up in the air. "Nothing left", Bart commented. They heard a noise, a spaceship was landing a few meters away. The three waited to see who came out. It was the Major, and Jed. "We come to get you"< Jed said holding his bionic arm up in salute. "I'm glad to see you alive", The major said, he smiled, "Now you owe me a strip show". He brayed at her. Marta returned the smile. "maybe I owe you one". "The Venusian? Jed asked. Bart shook his head slowly. "Zervax was very brave, a courageous soldier". They all got into the ship, and left for Andromeda. On arrival, Jed took off to his office to file a report. Marta turned towards Bart. "I owe the major one", she grinned, and "I'll be in a few". Bart shrugged "What ever". Bart continued, "I'll get us a room at the hotel Lux". Marta nodded, then left to see the major.

Bart checked into the hotel, An open credit line was left for him, and Marta. Bart checked into room 304, a luxury suite. It had tables, chairs, a desk, and a large floatation bed in the middle. Two hours later, there came a knock on the door. Bart opened the door, Marta standing there grinning at him. Not sure if he wanted to ask her, but he did. "What happened? Marta stepped in. "Nothing, really, she replied. She continued "He was a gentleman". "I did a slow strip for him, and gave him a little bump and grind show". Marta continued on, "I kissed him on the forehead, then left". She rolled her eyes up, and laughed. Bart grinned. Bart", she said softly, "I don't want any secrets between us". "Ok", Bart said, looking at her puzzled. "I know what you went through", she said quietly. She reached up behind her neck, and pulled. She was wearing a synth suit! Bart stared at her. Radiation burns marked her face, and breasts. "How…Bart stuttered. "Doesn't matter", she replied, approaching him. "We are what we are", she smiled, embracing him. "Yes we are", he said quietly. They embraced each other for a long time!

Chapter X

THE SHADOW MAN

I have seen him! God help me! He has become aware of me! In the multitude of crowds, I observed him, moving among therm. Spreading his violence and corruption everywhere. Touch here, a touch there. Mobs of people attacking each other. Rending and tearing at each other's flesh. He has been following me now for twenty four hours now. He has touched my girlfriend, Rita. She came at me with a butcher knife! She moved forward, cutting me once on the hand. It began to began to bleed. In defense, I gave her a shove, and she fell out the window, five stories down, the ground crushing her once attractive body. I Ran! I ran for my life! No one would believe me, that I hadn't committed murder. A police Officer stood at the corner, in his pressed blue uniform. The shadow man advanced towards him, touching him lightly on the shoulder. The officer grimaced, a horrible look sprouted on his clean shaven face. He fired several rounds at me. I saw the shadows' silhouette next to him, and it vanished. I ran in the opposite direction. I felt a sting in my left arm. I was hit with a grazing shot! Bleeding more, I wandered the city streets for hours. Then I spied it! A church! I approached it cautiously. A Catholic church! I hope I could be saved! Maybe the shadow man could not enter here. I went in, walking down the rows of pews. I approached the altar, kneeled down, and began to pray. A priest dressed in his robe and white collar, approached me. "Hi", he said, "I'm father Mike, "can I help you? Tears flowed down my cheeks.

Fumbling for the right words, I explained the situation to him. The priest listened, incredulously. "He's coming for me father", I said miserably. The father knelt down beside me, and we both prayed. "You're bleeding", he exclaimed. "Yes father, but right now we need to stop him". I answered. Father Mike reflected, "He may be able to enter the church." He sounds like a very strong and evil spirit. "You believe me? I asked. The priest replied, "There are many evil things in this material world", he made the sign of the cross. So we made a plan to defeat him. The priest ducked down between the vestibules, with a good size amount of holy water in the communion cup. I stood in front of the cross waiting. He came, making the church tremble, like an earthquake. It seemed to look around, spotting for trouble. Then it moved slowly towards me!

Menacing me! Half way down the pews, the priest stepped in front of it. He threw the cup of holy water on it, saying "Be gone evil spirit! Something sounded like a high pitched scream, and the shadow began to fade. Then it reached out its shadowy arms, and touched the priest. The priest spun around, a look of horror and hate on his face. I grabbed the cross with both hands.!

I sailed it across the room towards the two! It struck the priest, and landed on the shadow, pinning him to the ground. The priest hit the floor. I approached them cautiously.

I bent down, checking the priests' pulse. Nothing! The blow from the cross had killed him. A voice, sounding gravely and hollow spoke from the shadow. "Thank you", it said, "You have released me! "What! I shouted at him. The voice continued, "You have committed a sin, killing the priest! "Now I can move on". "It was an accident", I swore. "Never the less", the voice sounded weaker, I am gone, and you are cursed for committing a crime on holy ground". The shadow vanished in a cloud of dark, smelly smoke. I stood up, I could feel my human form changing, fading! Now, I thought, I am the shadow man! I left the church, gliding into the street, to mingle with the unsuspecting crowd. **Fear me!**